How I Killed My Grandmother

AND OTHER INCREDIBLE STORIES

How I Killed My Grandmother

AND OTHER INCREDIBLE STORIES

ANTHONY TOBIAS MENDELLE

APP
Alliance Publishing Press

ALLIANCE PUBLISHING PRESS

Published by Alliance Publishing Press Ltd
This paperback edition published 2021
Copyright © Alliance Publishing Press Ltd 2021
The moral right of the author has been asserted.

All rights reserved.

With the exception of attributed quotations, no part of this document may be reproduced or transmitted in any form or by any means, electronic, mechanical, photocopying, recording, or otherwise, without the prior written permission of Alliance Publishing Press Ltd.

ISBN: 978-1-83825-980-8
Typeset in Times New Roman

Book & Cover Design by **WORKSHOP**65.co.uk

BIOGRAPHY

Anthony Tobias Mendelle lived a long life and enjoyed a varied career. Born within the sound of Bow Bells in 1918, he was a quick, clever child who loved to tinker with all things mechanical.

He was conscripted into the army at 21 and served for six years throughout the Second World War, initially as a pilot posted to North Africa, and then by 1943 to Naples, Northern Italy, with the Army Education Corps. It was here that he got his first taste of broadcasting on the camp radio to the 1,000 troops stationed there. He also delivered lectures on subjects of his choosing three or four times a day, to 200–300 troops at a time. Anthony was then posted to the HQ of the AEC in Perugia, Southern Italy, where he ran the university until 1946, long after the war had ended.

He had married in 1942, and by the time he returned home was the father of Janet. After demobilisation he pursued an industrial career. He moved the family, now with the addition of son Paul, to run a factory in Wales where they stayed for several very happy years. In 1956, he returned to London to run an asbestos factory. With the gradual realisation that this was an extremely unhealthy mineral, Anthony was instrumental in the decision to close down the whole operation.

After retiring from industry, he continued to work, initially as a court reporter and then as practice manager for two firms of solicitors.

For most of his adult life, Anthony was a writer of plays, stories and books, based on his life and experiences. One of his stories was broadcast on BBC Radio Wales. In 2011, his novel The Chechen Assassination Plot, published under the name Anthony Tobias, was based on a true murder case he was involved in while running a criminal lawyer's practice.

When his wife of nearly 60 years, Nan, passed away he continued writing, cycling, and playing Scrabble and snooker, almost until his death in 2015, aged 97.

Anthony leaves a son and daughter, five grandchildren and eight great-grandchildren.

In memory of Tony and Nan Mendelle.
Loved, admired and remembered by their children,
grandchildren and great-grandchildren.

CONTENTS

HOW I KILLED MY GRANDMOTHER	11
THE WHORE OF BLACKHEATH	25
AUNT FLORRIE'S WHISTLE	39
ODYSSEY OF THE AMMONATIS	59
A STRIKING RESEMBLANCE	89
THE IMPRESARIO FROM LITTLE VENICE	95
AN IDEAL FOREMAN	121
THE SUMMING UP	139
MISTER NOBODY	151
CHE SARÀ, SARÀ	169

HOW I KILLED
MY GRANDMOTHER

Although it's almost 70 years since the tragic event took place, no one in the entire world is privy to my terrible secret. Now, at 80 years of age and probably due to expire before the millennium celebrations in the Dome at Greenwich, I feel it's time to confess my guilt.

I can't lie and say that killing my grandmother when I was 10 years old spoiled the rest of my life. I don't recall how old she was at the time, but she certainly looked old enough to die. One thing I have to make clear from the outset: the crime wasn't premeditated. At that age I didn't even know the meaning of the word. It may be a reflection on my flawed character that now I've made this momentous decision, I feel less motivated by the desire to expiate the sin and clear the slate with my creator than to observe the reactions of my family. The generations down to my great-grandchildren only know me as a high-minded law-abiding patriarch. I'd dearly like to see their faces as they read this confession.

For one thing, I'm going to describe places and customs as different from today's capital city as prints of Victorian life in horse-drawn London appeared to me, even though as a Cockney born and bred I walked the same city streets. It may seem unbelievable to today's generation, complaining as it does of the polluted environment with lead pouring into the atmosphere from petrol engines, but as a boy I picked my way to school across streets fouled with horse dung that in summer attracted blue bottle blow flies and didn't smell as sweet as daisies either. And at peak times, iron-wheeled brewers drays pulled by huge shire horses drove passengers mad as they plodded along tramlines slower than a childish amble. In those faraway days in the centre of the metropolis, it was frequently quicker to walk where you were going and be certain of passing rows of traffic held up at congested junctions on the way. Today's motorists may sigh with envy for the good old days of tranquil travel, but it was nothing like that when I was young. The golden age of nostalgic memory in my youth was for the days when everyone travelled by horse-drawn buses and there was no noise and clatter from electric trams.

I said I was cockney born and bred but that's not to give the impression my family and I were ill-spoken and coarse in our ways just because we lived within the sounds of St. Mary-le-Bow bells just outside the City of London. On the contrary, my parents regarded themselves as several cuts above others in the same district. In no way were we poor or underprivileged. For one thing, my father was a senior ticket-collector at Liverpool Street railway station and besides his gold-braided uniform, he and his family could travel free on the London North Eastern Railway as far as Southend-on-Sea. At school in Hoxton I wore knee-high socks, grey flannel trousers and a blazer with a badge on the breast pocket. And to and from the playground each day I also wore a pimple-top cap with the school colours sewn on its brim. There were boys in my class who wore dirty white plimsolls and had threadbare seats to their shorts, and at the midday break from lessons ate thick slices of bread spread with meat lard for their lunch, while I always had cheese sandwiches and an apple or a banana. Not that the differences between our circumstances bothered me at that age, but it brought out the beast in some. My mother was furious when one day I came home with my blazer torn as a result of a scuffle with a taunting classmate for being toffee-nosed. She referred to them as 'toe-rags' – an expression of social derision – and forbade me to walk the streets where those boys lived as if that measure alone would protect me from further schoolyard conflict. I also had other things that set me apart from my deprived contemporaries. I had a pair of roller skates for outdoor pleasure and a magic lantern complete with geographical slides for when the weather was bad. Less well-off neighbours must have thought my parents guilty of overindulging and spoiling me.

Though I was born at the closing stages of the Great War of 1914–1918, my father and his brothers were still reminiscing about the bloody conflict many years later. Much of their accounts of service on the Western Front made no impression on me – not even the deaths of members of the family who, had they survived, would have been my older cousins. As a sensitive young boy, as I was at the time, I didn't have it in me to shed tears for relatives I never knew. But it was a statement one day from my uncle Jack that changed everything for me and is at the root of this confession. It was to the effect that when the war was over and he was back from France on a troopship in one of London's docks, that in a defiant gesture against the military for the suffering and slaughter of his time in the trenches, he and others of like mind had thrown their weapons over the side of the ship into the River Thames.

The mistake adults make is to ignore the profound and permanent effect their conversation has on young imaginative minds. Though I was indifferent to the suffering and fate of relatives killed before I was born, I was fascinated by my uncle's tale of demobilisation and his act of defiance and the thought of all those rifles lying in the Thames was buried deep in my subconscious. It was a present from my father of a bicycle on my 10th birthday that was the catalyst that brought the story from the recesses to the surface of my mind. The bicycle was halfway to an adult model and opened up explorations far beyond the limits imposed on me by the small fairy cycle of my childhood. Now it was possible to journey beyond Moorgate and the Barbican when the city streets emptied as the workers left for home. The Tower of London and the Minories were within cycling distance and from there I could sit astride the Crimean cannons fronting the River Thames and watch Tower Bridge as it raised to let the cargo vessels pass through and lowered again for the waiting traffic and pedestrians to travel from north to south and vice versa.

Looking back, I realise now that I wouldn't be writing this confession if I hadn't been sitting by the river one day when the water was low and I saw a boy crouched barefoot in the mud, scraping at it with a piece of wood. Suddenly, the story of my uncle Jack came flooding back and I realised I wasn't alone in my knowledge of buried treasures. This boy too might have had an uncle on the troopship anchored in the pool of London just back from Flanders in 1918 and boasted to his contemporaries of throwing his arms and ammunition into the river as an act of defiance. He might at this very moment be digging in the mud for buried loot and I was desperate to get down and join him in the search for my uncle Jack's discarded rifle.

It may be wicked of me to infer it, but in a way my mother was indirectly responsible for the tragedy that befell her own parent. Her strict rules of upbringing influenced and inhibited my boyhood behaviour. It was perfectly all right to paddle in Southend-on-Sea's mud when we went there for a summer's day outing at LNER's expense, but it wasn't in order to walk barefoot in the streets of the City of London – certainly not in sight of the Tower of London and its famous bridge. And so I cycled in the direction of Wapping and searched for a place where I could down get to the ebb-tide river and walk along the mud until it squelched to my ankles and I was forced to take off my socks and shoes and, lace-tied, sling them round my shoulders. Unlike the boy I'd seen scouring the mud with a piece of driftwood, I hadn't anything in the way of a tool, and so I squatted and scratched at the mud with my fingers, combing it in the hope of uncovering a gun or a revolver or anything else that might have been thrown away by demobilised soldiers. I have no recollection now of how long I searched until the returning tide started lapping my ankles and I realised it was no longer safe to go on looking for my uncle Jack's rifle. All I had to show for my efforts was a piece of metal about three inches long, which was too wet to put in my pocket, so I had grasped in my muddied hand.

When I got back to the riverside steps where I'd left my bicycle, the boy I'd seen earlier on scraping away with his piece of wood was standing looking at it enviously. He was still barefoot, and he had holes in the seat of his ragged short trousers. He was what my mother would have termed a 'toe-rag'. He looked at me more with curiosity than friendliness.

'Fahnd anyfink?'

I shook my head, then as an afterthought held out the metal object. He looked at it scornfully.

'Tsa only a freeowfree. Ain't werf nuffink.'

I had no difficulty understanding his words but didn't know what it meant. He didn't wait for me to comment.

'Give yer a glarny forrit!'

The fact that he offered a glass marble for something he'd said wasn't worth anything was reason enough for me to want to keep it. Besides which, I had a bag full of multi-coloured marbles at home in my room. I shook my head and he stood watching as I put on my socks and shoes.

'Live rahnd eeyer?'

I shook my head again. I didn't want to accentuate the differences self-evident between us by replying to him. We spoke the same language, though a total stranger might have thought otherwise. Besides which, he looked rough and tough and my bicycle must have been a great temptation to him. He stood waiting till I got on the cycle and then with his free hand pushed the back of my saddle and gave me a flying start away from Wapping.

It was while pedalling furiously back to the comparative safety of Hoxton that I glanced down at my mud-caked socks and shoes and imagined my mother's wrath at the sight of them. I'd be compelled to explain the circumstances and watch her horrified expression as I admitted I'd ventured into dockland and walked barefoot in the Thames mud. Recriminations wouldn't stop there. She'd tell my father when he came home from work and he'd grumble at me for risking my bicycle being stolen by some ragamuffin after he'd saved up to buy me the birthday present in the first place. He was a man who regularly looked on the dark side of people's behaviour, talking about cheats who tried to pass him at the barrier without having paid their fare. Altogether the prospect of returning home in that state was too daunting to consider and so I decided to call in on my grandparents first who lived nearby in Shoreditch. I knew I was assured of a warm and criticism-free welcome from both. I was their first grandson and treated as someone special. Rather than cross-examined and reprimanded, I'd be given tea and biscuits and time to scrub by shoes and socks so that when I arrived back home my parents would never know about the riverside adventure looking for Uncle Jack's rifle. I'd hide the small metal 'freeowfree' the barefoot urchin had offered a glarny for and everyone would be happy. Being deceitful and cunning then, as now, was the natural process of growing up.

My welcome was as I expected. Both grandparents were pleasantly surprised to see me. My grandmother immediately went to the kitchen to make tea while my grandfather went to the garden shed to collect a handful of chestnuts. He knew roasting them on a shovel under the living room fire was a treat denied me at home. My mother was too house-proud and tidy to risk ash being sprinkled over her black-leaded hearth flanked by a coal scuttle and set of fire irons, and on the metal fender guard two matching brass frogs.

Without mentioning the true reason I'd called on them, and without waiting for comment on the state of my clothes, I went to the scullery and scrubbed my shoes and socks free of mud. When I'd done that I washed the metal object under the tap and was pleased when the caked dirt came away and I saw that it had a brass barrel one end and a white metal rim on the other. I had no idea what it was, but in its pristine state the 'freeowfree' looked to be worth more than just a glass glarny. I dried it on a towel, but water still seeped from the middle of it and so I wrapped it in my handkerchief to sop it up and put it in my trouser pocket.

When I went back into the living room my grandfather was enthusiastically raking the coals and spreading the chestnuts on the shovel before pushing them under the grate to roast.

I sat waiting for them to crackle as their skins split and the heat from the blazing fire burned against my legs and in a few minutes had penetrated the cloth of my trousers and I felt uncomfortable as the damp handkerchief started to dry out and scalded against my thigh. I shifted and twisted in my chair to make myself more comfortable, but the situation became worse and tiny spots of moisture appeared on the grey flannel cloth and slowly spread into a damp patch. Fortunately, both grandparents were too preoccupied to notice. My grandmother poured tea and my grandfather rotated the chestnuts with a pair of tongs. It was after we'd finished with both that the chance came for me to relieve the problem of the weeping metal object in my trouser pocket. While my grandmother took the tray to the kitchen to wash the crockery my father took the remains of the charred chestnut skins to the garden compost. When they were both out of the room I unwrapped the still wet 'freeowfree' and put it on the shovel and pushed it under the grate to dry.

Everything might have been all right if my grandfather hadn't returned from the garden and asked me to show him the bicycle I'd had for my 10th birthday, or even if my grandmother had taken longer to wash the cups, saucers and plates from tea. It was while he and I were standing in the front garden admiring the shiny black machine that we heard a noise like the crack of a thick thonged whip. My grandfather looked at me with a doleful expression, his enthusiasm for my bicycle suddenly gone.

'Sounds like she dropped one of her best plates on the kitchen floor. She'll be all cross with herself for that – and me too I shouldn't wonder.'

He turned to me, deeply apologetic.

'You don't want to see your gran all upset, do you, laddie?' He didn't wait for me to reply either way. 'I think it best you get off home.'

With that he waited till I mounted my bicycle then just like the barefoot boy at Wapping gave the back of my saddle a push for a good send-off. On reflection, as I've done many times thinking about the incident, I suppose it was reasonable for my grandfather to assess the situation as he did and assume the crack he heard while we stood in the garden was the shattering of a piece of valued crockery. He had no means of knowing the noise owed more to Woolwich than Stoke-on-Trent. Unlike my uncle Jack, he was too old to be called up for the Great War.

I didn't know what had happened till much later than night. I was asleep at the time. The first I knew something was seriously wrong was when for the first time in my life I heard my mother crying. Then my father came into my bedroom and told me that my grandmother was dead. He was very embarrassed when I started to cry. I'm not sure if being a senior ticket-collector at Liverpool Street station made him less sentimental than other men. I never saw him put an arm around my mother's shoulders in an affectionate hug, much less kiss her on the lips. For my part, I cried as much out of a sense of shock as grief. It seemed incomprehensible to me that someone who was alive and making me tea with a slice of Dundee fruit cake only a few hours before could now be dead. I suppose I must have cried myself to sleep and the next morning when I woke up I didn't think it right for me to say I was at my gran's cleaning up my socks and shoes before I came home the previous afternoon. For their part, neither of my parents seemed to expect me to say anything about the bereavement. My mother's eyes were red-rimmed and in a strange way I felt as embarrassed as my father had been with me the previous night. I couldn't find it in me to put my arms round her shoulders or kiss her on the cheek and say I was sorry her own mother was dead. I just left for school with my sandwiches in my satchel like any other day of the week. Perhaps if the truth be told, temperamentally I was my father's son in more ways than one.

I never heard mention at that stage of events, or even after the funeral, the question of a post-mortem. In 1927, sudden death was regarded as less of a tragic event than it is today. Working-class people could be expected to die without anyone suggesting there were suspicious circumstances to look into. My grandfather did tell the doctor he'd heard a noise coming from the house and when he'd come in from the garden he'd found her sitting in front of the fire and she was dead. I don't know if he mentioned the breaking of her favourite willow-pattern plate which he told me would have aggravated her. Anyway, my grandfather's GP confirmed that my grandmother must have suffered a massive heart attack as there were no signs of injury – no bruises or contusions to indicate violence against her. His diagnosis was unchallenged, and he signed the death certificate.

It wasn't until many years later, in fact, when I became a soldier at the outbreak of the Second World War in 1939, that I realised with horror that my grandmother's death might not have been as a result of a heart attack or even inconsolable grief over a broken plate from a favourite set of crockery, but that I personally might have been responsible. That when I was 10 years old and using her home to shield me against the wrath of my mother for having paddled in the Wapping mud, the bullet I'd put in the ash-can under the fire grate to dry may have shot out and the unexpected explosion caused her heart to stop with fright. The horrifying possibility became clear to me when I was issued with a uniform and Lee-Enfield rifle, both left-overs from the Great War of 1914. It was then for the first time I understood the Wapping urchin's variation of the English language. The 'freeowfree' he offered me a glass glarny for was the calibre of the brass-nosed bullet that went into the breech of a Lee-Enfield rifle. The metal object I'd scooped from the Thames mud while searching for my uncle Jack's rifle was a .303 shell – the ammunition used in the British Army in two world wars.

I suppose at that awful moment of realisation of personal culpability I should have been brave and admitted the possibility that I was responsible for my grandmother's death. My grandfather was still alive and living in my parents' home. He was very old but I'm sure he could have withstood the shock of my confession. After all, I was still his favourite grandson. But there was a war on, and I was a soldier helping to protect Great Britain from the enemy, even if in the days before the Blitz started all I was doing when out of barracks was guarding gasworks and other vital installations against German saboteurs and parachutists. It wasn't as if I was at risk of life or limb. With hindsight, I doubt if confession would have made a significant difference to what subsequently happened to me in my long and varied life. At no stage during it was I given to dwell on morbid thoughts. It's true my grandmother's death upset me at the time but it's against nature for a 10-year-old to sit and grieve for long. And though the realisation of the possibility of guilt was an overpowering reaction at the time when I was 21, its effect was fleeting, and the events of the war for the next six years took precedence over everything.

As I implied at the start of this confession, recounting this childhood incident is more a question of relieving conscience than seeking forgiveness. It most certainly isn't fear of the consequences when I die and have to answer to my maker for my life's sins. On reflection, I don't know that anything that followed the 70 years since that fateful incident would have been different if, for instance, I'd accepted the glarny from the Wapping toe-rag in exchange for the 'freeowfree', or even cycled straight home and been bold enough to face my mother's outrage at the sight of my muddy shoes instead of stopping off at my grandparents in Shoreditch to clean off the Wapping mud.

One thing I do know for certain, and that is from that day to this I can't bear the sight, smell or taste of roasted chestnuts. Even a glimpse of a tin shovel, like my grandfather used to place the shiny mahogany brown shell nuts on before resting it under the blazing coals in the Victorian-type fireplace grate, transports me back in time.

One final comment on this nostalgic reminiscence. Not long after my grandmother's funeral, my grandfather came to live with us. He didn't bring much with him. Working-class people didn't have a lot in the way of furniture or valuable possessions in 1927. One piece he did trundle round on a wheelbarrow from Shoreditch to our house in Hoxton was a glass-fronted china cabinet. I remember my mother saying that, like her own mother, it was a favourite piece of hers too. I can hear her now as she stood and admired it with all the pieces of china set out on the glass shelves.

'It looks good there, Dad. Just like it was in your parlour. Specially the willow-pattern tea set. Pity there's one plate missing.'

THE WHORE OF BLACKHEATH

I was 5 years old when a major crisis struck my family. I don't mean involving me personally. I was the first grandson and regarded as someone special by all my relatives. I mean a major crisis involving my parents, grandparents, uncles and aunts.

Not that at that tender age I knew which family was affected. My grandparents' identity was more a matter of geography than personality. When my parents referred to their respective homes before they were married, it was never by name. It was either East Ham or Greenwich. At alternate weekends we went from our house in Hoxton to one or the other. The journey to East Ham was only a short bus ride away but to Greenwich it was more exciting because it took us either over the River Thames on the Woolwich ferry or under it through Blackwall Tunnel.

How I knew things were different from our usual visit to Greenwich was the fact that when we got there everyone was sitting in the front parlour instead of in the kitchen. I can't pretend that I could tell from the looks on their faces that they were waiting for us to arrive before discussing the crisis, but that's what they were doing.

Unlike parents who protest to everyone they never have favourites among their children, of all the relatives at East Ham or Greenwich the one I liked most was my uncle Alec. For one thing, compared to the others he was young. He carried me on his shoulders, pretending to drop me when my head was inches from the ground, and bought me ice-cream cornets. Once he took me to a music hall theatre. I clapped when the drums rolled and acrobats did their tricks, but I fell asleep on his lap when a woman sang and danced with her bloomers showing. It was much later that I realised it wasn't surprising my uncle Alec was always laughing and jolly. At the time of the family crisis he was the only one in the room who wasn't married.

As I said about parents claiming not to have favourites among their children, they also believed that when they were in company children should be seen and not heard. As a result, they totally underestimated what they were taking in as they sat playing with their toys, quiet, well behaved, and a credit to their upbringing. Mine were no different, otherwise they wouldn't have let me stay in the room that Saturday afternoon in Greenwich.

With my baby sister fast asleep in her carry-cot and me on the floor building a house with bricks, they felt free to talk about the crisis within the family. That is, everyone except Uncle Alec. He just sat looking down at me playing with my toys and saying nothing. It was the first time I'd seen him without a smile on his face. Not that anyone else in the room that afternoon looked cheerful.

It's strange when I think back to the family sitting hunched and intense in that Greenwich parlour, the image I retain is of a blurred faded photograph. Perhaps it's natural for memories of long-dead relatives to become indistinct. If it is, it doesn't explain why one remains bright and clear even after 70 years. That's how it is in the snapshot of my mind; everyone that afternoon, including my parents, fuzzy and indistinct, except for Uncle Alec. He still stands out bright and clear.

It was my father who started proceedings. When he spoke to my uncle he sounded angrier than I'd heard him before.

'You do realise you're being taken for a ride?'

My mother echoed my father as she always did.

'Harry's right, Alec. As your eldest brother he knows what he's talking about.'

The fact that my mother spoke was a signal for all the aunts to pipe up. I couldn't make out everything they said but I heard the words 'scheming bitch' several times. I didn't know what a scheming bitch was but even while concentrating on trying to keep my brick house from falling down I could tell that it couldn't be anything nice.

'You're a young fool. You don't know what day it is.'

When my grandfather spoke for the first time he sounded grave. I couldn't grasp why he said Uncle Alec didn't know what day it was. I thought all grown-ups knew that.

'There's 13 years between you. Thirteen years! You're 18 and she's 31.'

At this information, my father became so agitated he got up and his chair knocked my bricks all over the floor. He didn't seem to notice, or if he did he didn't say sorry. I didn't cry or make a fuss because Uncle Alec leant down and gathered them together for me.

Then it was my grandmother's turn. She too sounded serious.

'When you're still a young man she'll be an old woman. You understand what that will mean?'

If my uncle did understand what it meant he didn't say so. Not even when the aunts echoed my grandmother.

'Married to an old woman. He's got to be mad.'

Suddenly, everything went quiet. I looked up. My father was carefully folding a newspaper. When it was quite small he held it in front of my uncle's face.

'Read what it says there.'

Alec scanned it briefly and looked away. My father continued to stare at him then began to read aloud.

'Blackheath's fight against vice. On Monday night, several women were arrested on the Common and will appear in the magistrates' court later this week charged with soliciting. A police spokesman said it was their intention to keep the town free of indecent behaviour.'

He put the paper in his pocket as if to protect the ladies of the family from reading the news item for themselves but gave no thought to me hearing about soliciting and indecent behaviour on Blackheath Common.

'Your bitch is on the game!'

The remark puzzled me out of my preoccupation with the bricks and I looked up at him. I knew what games were. I played them at school when I came out of the classroom. But what game the bitch of Blackheath was playing was a mystery to me.

My father waited for him to reply, but Alec stayed silent.

'How far gone is she supposed to be?'

'Two months.'

They were the first words Alec had uttered. It was my mother as usual who repeated them.

'Two months? Let her get rid of it. That would be best for everyone.'

'No!'

It was the defiant way Alec shouted that had a dramatic effect. Instead of looking angry, the family became resigned and left it to my father to speak out for them.

'You do realise if you go through with this it will be too embarrassing to bring the woman home here to Greenwich? I don't claim to speak for your brothers and sisters or their partners, but as far as my wife and I are concerned, neither you nor she will be welcome at Hoxton.'

While my grandparents nodded approval, there was a chorus of assent from the rest of the family. My mother decided my father's statement about the homes of Greenwich and Hoxton being denied to his youngest brother was an official end to the crisis meeting. She went to the carry-cot and started to change my baby sister's napkin. One of the aunts got up and said she was going to make tea and there was a general movement out of the room. It got so crowded I had to abandon my bricks and see if I could find something else to play with. I looked at Alec staring dejectedly at the floor and left to rummage in a hall cupboard that was full of interesting things. When I came back with a box of dominoes, everyone had disappeared. I went into the kitchen where they were sitting drinking tea and still talking about him and the bitch from Blackheath.

I can't be sure who suggested my father went and tried to talk her out of things because appealing to young Alec was a waste of time.

'You're the eldest, Harry. Go and speak to her. If it comes to it, pay her off. After all, that's what she's used to. We'll all put our hands in our pockets.'

Everyone was in agreement.

'He's 18 years old, for God's sake. How does he know she's two months gone – just because she says so?'

'Or even that it's his. Being on the game, it could be anyone's.'

'You go there, Harry, and get the whore to lay off the kid. You can do it.'

It was obvious that all my aunts and uncles, even including my favourite uncle Alec, were just like my parents, ignoring the fact that their 5-year-old nephew was taking in and registering every word they said, and even though 'bitch' and 'whore' were terms I'd certainly never heard before and couldn't know what they meant, I knew instinctively they stood for something bad.

One after the other they were enthusiastic at the suggestion that my father visit the wicked woman and talk her out of marrying young Alec, which if she did would banish him from the family and cause unhappiness all round. I saw my father look to my mother as if seeking approval, but she was preoccupied with covering herself up as she breast-fed my baby sister.

In recalling events of more than 70 years ago, I can't pretend that from that day onwards I was intensely curious to know the outcome of my father's visit to Blackheath. I didn't know if he had offered her cash to 'get rid of it' and how deep my uncles put their hands in their pockets to help out. I didn't know whether Alec had married the woman 'on the game' and 'two months gone'. I was kept in that state of ignorance from that crisis meeting onwards and there was never another family gathering at Greenwich to discuss the subject.

Instead there was another family crisis 16 years later, but this time none of the uncles, aunts and grandparents were invited from Greenwich to gather in our front parlour or have tea afterwards in our kitchen. No one from East Ham was invited either, even though they were much nearer. It was a very private family crisis.

It took place in the summer of 1939. At the time I was a 21-year-old conscript doing six months' National Service in an army camp in Dorset. I didn't know the reason my parents wrote and asked me to come home, only that it was to discuss a serious family situation, but I applied for and was granted weekend leave and a return travel pass to London.

When I got home it transpired that my 16-year-old sister, who had recently left school and was now working full-time in a local factory, had missed two menstrual periods. Flooding back from my earliest recollection was my father's query of another female in the same condition. Like the whore of Blackheath, my sister was 'two months gone'!

The family reunion that weekend was not the happiest of occasions. My father in particular was less dominant than when he'd ranted at his youngest brother for his outrageous behaviour. My mother as usual seemed calmer and more in control. Thinking back, I've no idea if either of them considered for a moment the irony of their 16-year-old daughter, watched over at home by doting parents and at school by devoted nuns till she left at 15, had now created a crisis not dissimilar from that caused by my uncle Alec. I glanced at her sitting huddled and dejected, staring down at the floor. Again, the past came flickering back with the image of my uncle staring down at his feet while my mother's rasping voice called out about the woman of his choice.

'Let her get rid of it!'

My thoughts were broken into by that same harsh voice.

'Your father and I talked to your sister about not going through with it, but she's being very obstinate.'

I didn't know how old the man was who'd impregnated her, and I didn't feel it my business to ask. Maybe at the back of my mind was the fear that like the women of vice referred to in the *Blackheath Gazette*, she too might have been 'on the game'. Unlike a 5-year-old, as a man who'd reached his majority, I knew the game wasn't anything like marbles or tag. But whatever the strangeness of the situation, one thing my sister had in common with the bitch who'd 'hooked' my uncle was that she was equally determined to bear the child in her womb.

Again my mother's tart voice interrupted my thoughts.

'We've had a word with your aunt at Canvey. Your sister can stay there till the baby's born. Then we'll bring it up as your father's and mine. No one else need know.'

The statement was definitive. I wondered why I'd been summoned to hear the arrangement when I could have been told as much in a letter. My father didn't seem overenthusiastic. Maybe it was the thought of having his first grandchild brought up as his own. Or that the deceit on family and friends of procreating after a lapse of 16 years somehow cast a slur on his virility. At the time he was 44 years old.

For my part, I felt detached and uninvolved, much as I did as a 5-year-old in Greenwich when I concentrated on building my brick house on the parlour floor while the question of Alec's problem raged about me. The fact that by the time I finished my service and came back to Hoxton my sister would be on Canvey Island made the problem too remote to upset me. I was a young man, well away from family responsibilities and nosy neighbours. Blandford had more immediate priorities for me than either Hoxton or Canvey.

I don't remember if I thought of my parents as hypocrites for dealing with the situation of their daughter's unwanted pregnancy more rationally than they had with the woman of Alec's choice. Thinking about the irony of the situation now, I realise in both circumstances they were doing what all families do under dramatic circumstances: stand together to protect one of their own. But even had I been reflective and philosophical at the time of the crisis and pointed out the inconsistency of their behaviour, these domestic issues would have paled into insignificance. It was only months later that war was declared against Germany and there was never to be another family reunion at Hoxton to discuss any problem ever again.

In common with other conscripts who'd spent months drilling and route-marching, in September 1939 I was considered militarily efficient and sent to France as part of the British Expeditionary Force. Kitted out in khaki tunic and Lee-Enfield rifle, I looked more like a soldier of the First World War than a combatant of the second. I didn't know at the time that I was to stay in uniform several years longer than any infantryman who survived the bloody slaughterhouse of 1914-1918.

Under the circumstances, I wasn't called upon to distinguish myself in battle. My division was in the gap of Flanders, west of the French Maginot Line, and when German Panzers breached it we were ordered back to Calais. The relief at not being killed or injured was offset by the humiliation of marching back the way we'd come. Home again in 1940, we were reissued battle-dress and gaiters instead of tunic and puttees and posted to the Orkneys to stop the Germans coming through Scotland and defeating us that way.

The following six months were tedious. In the army you're either bored or scared. Even when Goering's Luftwaffe started blitzing London and other English cities I was still languishing safe and sound in my Highland billet. The only news of interest I received from my parents during that time was that my sister had miscarried in her fourth month, and because of the air raids in Hoxton was staying on with my aunt on Canvey Island.

It was a few days before Christmas 1943 that I was sent for by my company commander. I was now stationed with my battalion in North Africa. This time we were marching forwards instead of backwards. I'd never been sent for or spoken to by him personally before. He told me in a kindly and sensitive way that my parents had been killed by a doodlebug falling in Hoxton and they were buried in the local cemetery. There was no mention of being granted compassionate leave. Perhaps there was no purpose travelling back to England from Tunisia just to gape at a hole in the ground where they'd lived and died.

A letter did arrive some weeks later from my sister saying a number of aunts and uncles had come to the funeral, but it was raining as they stood by the graveside and she didn't recognise all of them sheltering under umbrellas. They dispersed afterwards, and she went straight back to Canvey. I can't in recollection say when I read that letter if I wondered whether my uncle Alec had been among the mourners, and if so, whether he was alone or with someone. I'd never mentioned him or my childhood remembrances of the incident at Greenwich with my sister. There was no call to do so then or ever since.

It may seem self-evident to say that I survived the war, but I was fortunate in that I did so with all my limbs and faculties intact. After almost seven years in the service of King George VI, I was demobilised and returned to civilian life in 1946. I stayed with my grandparents in East Ham until such time as I met my wife and from then on did what everyone else did with their lives – got a job, earned a living and raised a family.

The war had done more to me than kill my parents. The Greenwich grandparents had died of natural causes. There was no longer a venue or a desire for aunts and uncles to meet. Except for hearing when one or the other passed away, I didn't see or meet them from one year to the next. In time my wife and I became the weekend meeting place for our children and their offspring. I don't know if they referred to the visits as 'going to Weybridge'. My grandchildren had weird names and catchphrases for us. They were nothing as straight forward and identifiable as 'Greenwich' or 'East Ham'. But as I watched them playing with their electronic toys and computer games I had no doubt they were taking in everything that was being said around them as I'd done at their tender ages.

It was an unusual event by any standard that brought my childhood flooding back to me with startling vividness. One day a young man arrived at our riverside home with a bundle under his arm. He was too presentable to be asking for charity or selling encyclopaedias. He addressed me by my Christian and surname together, which was surprising, and asked if he could come in.

Once inside, he came straight to the point by unrolling the parcel he was carrying and spreading it on the floor. It was a family tree, elaborately drawn and very detailed.

'I've been compiling it for several years, tracing my ancestors as far back as I can. I discovered one of them in a 16th century Norfolk church register. It's become more than a hobby with me – it's an obsession.' He was very enthusiastic and very proud of his scroll. 'I keep discovering relatives I've never heard of before. That's how I learned about you here in Weybridge.'

I must have looked as surprised and perplexed as I felt. I racked my brains to think which of my parents' folks originated from Norfolk, but I couldn't recall either of them mentioning anyone further away than East London. His voice cut across my thoughts.

'It was when I came to my grandmother on my father's side that I came across your name for the first time. It's exciting finding new relatives. It's opened a whole new world to me.'

The enthusiasm of the young man in his 30s was infectious. The mention of his grandmother focused my mind more clearly. Of all the uncles and aunts I knew of alive or dead from East Ham or Greenwich, none had a grandson who would only recently have discovered his family north or south of the Thames. There was only one person he could possibly be referring to and that was Uncle Alec. My pulse rate quickened. Was the dreadful secret of the past to be revealed at last? Was a skeleton to come rattling out like a ghost to haunt and torment me? I kept my voice from trembling.

'Where was your grandmother from?'

'Norwich in Norfolk. All her kinfolk were. She was quite a character. Almost lived to a hundred.'

'Did she ever live in London?'

He shrugged.

'I wouldn't know. She didn't talk much about herself.'

'What about your grandfather? Do you remember him?'

'I never knew him. He died before I was born.'

'You found out he was from London? You know that for certain?'

'It was on the Norwich church register – and their marriage certificate. That and the dates of their birth. She outlived him even though she was much older.'

'Much older?'

'My parents said they were living proof that happy marriages aren't necessarily between people of the same age. From everything I heard about them they were very happy together.'

The young man stayed for the rest of the evening, wanting to know all about the East Ham and Greenwich families. He seemed genuinely interested, even though there was nothing remarkable about any of them. I told him all I knew except the one dark secret.

'You've given me enough information to keep this tree growing for years. Next time we meet I'll need a bigger floor than this to spread it out.'

He was being very tactful, suggesting that after more searching and adding to his genealogical record I'd still be around to study and enthuse about it with him.

After he left I sat mulling over the quirk of fate that a complete stranger, who'd never set eyes on my favourite uncle but discovered him through meticulous searches of his own family, should be the one to tell me of his life and death in Norfolk. The fact that he didn't know whether his late 98-year-old grandmother had ever spent part of her life in London made the past more intriguing for me than before and stirred long-forgotten memories of the last time I saw Alec staring down at me as a 5-year-old child, his usually laughing face clouded over and sad.

The mystery remained whether my father's visit to Blackheath to rescue his 18-year-old brother from entering into a misbegotten marriage had succeeded, with him paying her to abort her pregnancy and leave Alec free to mature into manhood, or that in spite of all the threats, appeals and bribery, Uncle Alec continued to defy him and the family and married the street-walker who reformed her life and his by returning to her roots in Norfolk and leading a blameless and happy life with him till he died.

In the final analysis I know that no matter how long that

young man's scroll grows and how many ancestors he adds to the branches of the family tree, one thing is absolutely certain: no one is ever going to know for sure whether Uncle Alec married the whore of Blackheath.

AUNT FLORRIE'S WHISTLE

The final moment of truth for Miss Florence Merryman's independent way of life came at a most inconvenient time. It was lying on her stomach, blocking the front entrance of her Surbiton flat. She'd been warned repeatedly that she might fall and not be able to get up again, and if that happened she could die from shock, hypothermia, hunger and thirst – or all four at the same time.

It wasn't that the 90-year-old spinster with all her faculties was obstreperous or obstinate towards her family. She'd outlived her contemporaries and attended funerals of others. It was only when implored to give up residence in Surbiton and be looked after by carers that she dug her metaphoric heels in and threatened to leave her wealth to Battersea Dogs Home in retaliation for the unfeeling assault on her independence.

In the end, when the dreaded crisis came, it wasn't as a result of appeals to reason or accepting the inevitable. It came because she forgot a whistle she routinely wore on a lanyard around her neck to summon help in the event of an emergency. It was her lifeline to independence. Without it she'd no means of alerting anyone of her desperate plight, lying prone and helpless, blocking her own front door. She was indeed facing the moment of truth. If she did survive the shocks to her system, what argument could she offer against giving up independence and retiring to an establishment for middle-class genteel folk? That was the family's verbal camouflage for an old people's home conveniently close to them in Surrey where they could take it in turns to make dutiful visits and keep alive the prospect of maintaining the advantage over the canines in Battersea.

Rescue came before the four horsemen of the apocalypse could claim Miss Merryman. As he pushed a clutch of circulars through her letter box, the postman saw a pair of feet sticking out where they shouldn't. He called the porter who opened the door by unceremoniously pushing her to one side for the paramedics to stretcher and take her to an ambulance, despite her demand to be carried to her bedroom. Whether she liked it or not, Aunt Florrie was hospital bound and that was the end of it.

For a woman with a strong constitution and even stronger temperament, shock hardly registered, and the arm she broke when she fell was a low hurdle to clear on the route to survival. Once the plaster was removed, Florence Merryman was discharged from the local hospital and on the pretext that she was going to a convalescent home till fully recovered, transported to a retirement home in Surrey. There was no mention of not going back to her flat at some time in the future. This was in case the statement brought on delayed shock. It was the risk that when being told she was to be permanently resident at the home she might create such a fuss that she would be unsuitable for the administrators of the establishment, in which case she'd have to be taken back to Surbiton and other complicated arrangements made to look after her there.

The Lady Beauchamp's residential home in Surrey was once the private manse of a wealthy family which fell on hard times with porous slate and leaking plumbing. On a sunny day it was a delight for visitors to walk around admiring the gardens before driving away and thanking their stars they weren't staying inside with the collection of semi-senile genteel folk residents.

Fortunately for the relatives, nature came to their aid. Aunt Florrie's short-term memory, faltering before the fall, deteriorated rapidly after it. Not only was memory of her helpless collapse gone from her mind, but current events were failing to register.

'What am I doing here?'

'You fell and cracked your elbow. Don't you remember being in hospital with a cast on your arm?'

Her voice was sharp as she looked gimlet-eyed at the group of elderly men and women sitting around her in various degrees of somnolent vagueness.

'Are they all here on convalescence? Some look half dead to me!'

'They're recuperating, Aunt Florence.'

It was collectively agreed among the family that calling their aunt Florrie was all right in Surbiton but not in Lady Beauchamp's private residential home in Surrey. If she noticed the formality she made no comment.

'I don't remember being in hospital with a broken arm. I was never in hospital before. I've always been fit. And I've got all my own teeth.'

The statements concerning her health were true. If there was any physical vanity in her, it was focused on her molars. It was a source of great pride that she'd never brushed her teeth, only rubbed them with a cloth.

'How long have I got to stay here?'

'Till you're strong enough to hold a walking stick. You don't want to fall again. You'd not be able to walk on your own. You'd be confined to a wheelchair.'

The warning was ignored as an irrelevance.

'When did I fall?'

'Two weeks ago.'

'Where?'

'In the hallway – blocking the front door.'

'Didn't I blow my whistle for help?'

'No, Aunt Florence, you didn't blow your whistle for help. You couldn't blow your whistle. You weren't wearing it.'

She bridled as if accused of some indecent impropriety.

'Rubbish! I always wear it round my neck.'

'You forgot the day you fell.'

'Forgot? Nonsense! There's nothing wrong with my memory. I can remember back to when I was 4.'

When she disagreed with anyone she sat bolt upright in her chair and rocked from side to side like a metronome. For a 90-year-old arthritic woman it was a remarkably expressive movement. The body language combined with a fierce expression could prove intimidating, particularly to people of a less assertive nature. Though it was undeniable she could recall the past in detail, gone from her mind were events of yesterday.

'The fact remains, Aunt Florence, you forgot to wear your whistle and if it hadn't been for the postman who sent for the porter you might not be alive today. Incidentally, we've thanked them and bought each a present.'

***

As the time went by, Miss Merryman remained hostile to her stay in the Surrey home and the relationship between her and the staff was strained. It wasn't just due to the fact that she was more alert and articulate than the majority of residents in varying stages of physical and mental decrepitude. It was her accompanying attitude that being 90 years old entitled her to priority of attention regardless of the fact that her tenure was only weeks long while others had been there for years. Tolerance and patience were notably absent from her personality, as the administrators at Lady Beauchamp pointed out tactfully to visiting members of Aunt Florence's family.

It was the affair of the seating arrangements in the conservatory that demonstrated, temperamentally and psychologically, that Aunt Florrie had crossed the dividing line between single-mindedness and strength of character into wilful cantankerousness and unreasonable obstinacy.

There was nothing special about the furniture in the large glasshouse overlooking the garden where residents regularly sat in the warmth and dozed between breakfast and lunch and again from tea to supper till it was time to go to bed and sleep all night. The armchair in the room that took Florence's fancy had a blue cushion just like her favourite chair at home in Surbiton. She had a thing about blue. The chair had long been recognised by residents and staff alike as the seat of a favoured guest referred to only by initials – Mrs. C.-B. from Belgravia.

Mrs. Olivia Christie-Bowler had for years, before infirmity overtook her, resided in Sloane Square. She was very highly regarded at Lady Beauchamp as the epitome of a well-bred Englishwoman. She was not only wealthy but distantly related to a lord who'd married into money, not simply to maintain a lifestyle befitting an impecunious peer but to uphold the British tradition of hereditary aristocracy. The administrators in particular appreciated the fact that her titled relative regularly came to visit her. On the face of it, Mrs. Olivia Christie-Bowler, formerly of Belgravia, had every social and material advantage over Miss Florence Merryman from Surbiton. Besides which, she was a mere youngster of 70, but not so strong-willed and robust as the spinster 20 years her senior.

In the weeks since Florence's arrival, neither had exchanged a word of greeting or acknowledged each other's presence either in the conservatory or elsewhere in the home. Their mutual antipathy was instinctive. One fateful day, Miss Merryman took it upon herself to occupy Mrs. C.-B.'s favourite chair in the conservatory well before her morning arrival.

The details of the ensuing confrontation were related to family visitors by Florence without shame or conscience. If anything she was arrogant and smug as she recounted the furore and shocked reactions that resulted from her unseemly aggressive behaviour.

'I just sat there and refused to move!'

'But Aunt Florrie, staff told you Mrs. Christie-Bowler had sat in that chair for years. Everyone recognised it as hers. Out of respect they all left it for her.'

'More fools them. It's the best seat in the conservatory. It's time others had a turn. Besides, she's colour blind. She can't tell red from green.'

'She just gave up and let you sit there?'

'She could hardly pick me up and put me somewhere else.'

'Staff said a colonel came and ticked you off.'

She bridled at the mention of his rank.

'If he'd laid a finger on me I'd have hit him with my stick. Anyway, they shouldn't have men and women living together in convalescent homes. It's indecent.'

And so Florence took and kept possession of the favourite blue-cushioned armchair, adding insult to injury by turning it round so that it faced the blue lavender bushes instead of overlooking the rose garden. It was not long after this provocative incident with Mrs. C.-B. that there was a second embarrassing encounter, this time in the dining room. Since the victory of the conservatory, Florence had taken to pouring salt on Mrs. C.-B.'s wounds by sitting at the same table and throughout the meal fixing her with a defiant stare so as to cause her the maximum discomfiture.

The fare served at lunchtime was traditionally English, as befitted a Surrey county home. The crisis that befell Mrs. C.-B. on this particular occasion was due to the fact that when she opened her mouth to take the first portion of boiled beef and pease pudding, she realised she'd forgotten to wear her dentures. Her cry of dismay was involuntary and at the sound of it Florence looked up and caught sight of her gaping jaws and toothless gums. Her triumphant cry of delight could be heard by everyone in the dining room.

'Look at her! The lady from Belgravia's got no teeth!'

It was from that crushing incident onwards that Mrs. C.-B.'s haughty and imperious bearing declined, and for a while – not out of affection but fear of her sharp tongue and overbearing manner – Miss Florence Merryman of Surbiton replaced Mrs. Olivia Christie-Bowler as the force majeure at Lady Beauchamp's Surrey home for genteel folk.

But reputations in the home, like lives themselves, were transient. So it was that Florence Merryman's reign of supremacy continued only until the arrival of Arthur J. Hartley, Professor Emeritus of history at London University and former BBC television personality.

A.J.H., as he was known, outranked everyone by virtue of his intellect and personality, even though by the time of his arrival at Lady Beauchamp's he couldn't remember what the present scene was about let alone the past. Nonetheless, in spite of suffering from Alzheimer's disease, the cachet of his former fame as a TV lecturer and instantly recognisable to millions of viewers whether interested in history or not meant he was regarded as the home's most illustrious resident. A.J.H. was in a category way above that of either Miss Merryman or Mrs. C.-B.

It went without saying that the effect on Florence of being usurped as the home's cynosure was to stir emotions of fierce jealousy. At A.J.H.'s first enfeebled appearance in the conservatory, assisted by a carer, she went on the attack.

'I saw you once on the telly.'

His wry smile, once a familiar expression to viewers, now gave him a vague and vacuous look.

'That was good of you.'

'I couldn't understand a word you said. Did you get paid for talking that gibberish?'

'Gibberish? Paid? When was that?'

Florence could see the former historian was suffering from advanced senility. She was relentless.

'Are you all there? You don't look like you've got all your marbles to me.'

The carer standing by his wheelchair came to his aid.

'Professor A.J.H. is here to relax from his busy schedule, not to discuss his previous public appearances.'

There was no nurse in the residential home who could fob off Miss Merryman and expect to get away with it. The head-shaking, seat-squirming danger signals of attack were in motion.

'How old are you – 21 or 22? I'm over 90 and you can't tell me he's here to relax. He'll not be going on telly again that's for sure. He's gone in the head – that's why you're looking after him!'

Whether or not A.J.H. understood a word she said or simply

didn't like the look or sound of her, the famous personality never set foot in the conservatory again with or without a nurse. He never appeared in the dining room either, eating all his meals in his room. The virago from Surbiton had seen him off at his first appearance and she was once more in the ascendant. It wasn't to last, however, and no one could have foreseen the manner and end of her short-lived victory.

Nemesis came in the form of Mrs. Vera Bransby late of Peckham Rye. It wasn't so much that the 99-year-old widow was remarkably preserved that impressed the inhabitants of the residential home, it was her force of personality and resolute action that swiftly won their collective esteem. At her first morning appearance in the conservatory she took occupation of the blue-cushioned armchair and turned it away from the lavender bushes and round to face the rose garden. When Florence Merryman came into the room and stood glaring white-faced with rage, she just sat staring out at the garden and refused to budge. Up till that critical moment the spinster's ferocious expression and acid-sharp tongue were enough to intimidate the staunchest opponent.

'I'll have you know that's my place. I sit there.'

Not only did Vera Bransby remain seated, she made no reply. Instead, with an exaggeratedly calm manner, she examined both arms of the chair then swivelled to scrutinise behind her. When she was done she sat back and looked up with a bland and innocent expression.

'I can't see anyone's name written on it.'

Florence's hands holding her Zimmer frame twitched so uncontrollably the front legs of the metal support beat a tattoo on the tiled floor.

'Everyone in the conservatory knows I sit there.'

'No one said anything to me. They couldn't do. I was here before anyone. Anyway, it was facing the wrong way.'

'It was facing the way I wanted.'

'Well, take another one and put it there.'

The biter was bit! On her very first appearance in the conservatory the newly arrived diminutive resident from Peckham had taken possession of Florence's prized piece of furniture and maintained squatter's rights. It was a defeat and humiliation for the spinster from Surbiton. As far as the other residents were concerned it was the most satisfying episode in the battle for ascendancy and the brief but dramatic confrontation did more to stir their sluggish circulations than throwing medicine balls or taking part in old-time dancing.

As if commandeering the coveted seat was not insult enough, Mrs. Vera Bransby held court in the conservatory, attracting others besides the usual residents who came to listen to her reminiscences. She thrived on the attention while Florence Merryman just sat listening to her tales with a clenched jaw and grim expression. Even though her chair was half turned from her adversary, there was no way she could avoid hearing the lifetime recollections of the 99-year-old widow.

'I was standing with Sylvia Pankhurst at Tattenham Corner when Emily Davison ran out in front of the horses at the Epsom Derby. That was in 1913. We went there to kick up a fuss. We didn't think she'd get herself killed.'

Few of the residents had met a celebrity who could relate first-hand accounts of the suffragette martyr a year before the start of the Great War in 1914.

'Sylvia's mother Emmeline blew up Lloyd George's villa in 1912. She got three years in Holloway prison for that but they let her out when she went on hunger strike and nearly died.

I tell you there's nothing today's feminists can teach us old women. We started the whole thing.'

She relished the chance to relive her moments of glory.

'We chained ourselves to railings and smashed windows. The Government gave up in the end. We got the vote in 1918. During the General Strike in 1926 I was a conductress on a tram. It went from Kennington to the Elephant and Castle. A week that lasted. I wished it had gone on longer. I liked punching tickets. But as usual the men caved in.'

There was no resident or member of staff at the home to compare with her memory. Even Mrs. C.-B. from the other side of the social divide and at 70, a mere fledgling compared to Vera Bransby approaching her century, was intrigued to sit and listen to her recounting her past adventures.

'Women today don't know what struggle is. We didn't go round burning bras to prove our independence. We didn't wear them. We wrapped ourselves flat so that policemen had nothing to grab hold of when they arrested us.'

No listener was old enough to have created civil mayhem before the First World War, and all in the cause of getting women the same voting rights as men. Such was her ability to hold sway; it went unquestioned whether this ex-convict and one-time scourge of governments was a suitable resident at Lady Beauchamp's home for genteel folk, seeing that by her own accounts she was far from being ladylike. But even had there been a complaint the administrators would have ignored it, not simply because she paid her fees the same as the rest, but that as the star attraction, the former firebrand from Peckham Rye was infinitely preferable to the shrewish spinster from Surbiton who'd held court in the conservatory before her.

And for good measure, just to prove she wasn't buried in

the past, Vera Bransby was also ready to pronounce on the contemporary scene.

'Women have come a long way since my day. They've got their own back on men all right. They've even given them up as husbands and fathers, but fat lot of good it's done them. Sometimes I wonder if the struggle was worth it.'

Not that anyone was prepared to question the founding suffragette's attitudes to modern-day love and life. That is, no one except Miss Florence Merryman. She was ready to question everything about her loathed adversary. But in the absence of anyone in the home willing to listen to her viperish comments she had to wait till a member of family arrived to vent her spleen. When she did, she raised her voice so that others might hear exactly what she had to say.

'How do we know the woman chained herself to railings? Just because she says she did?'

She rocked her shoulders and squirmed in her seat with pent-up resentment.

'Anyone as old as she is can say what they like to gullible people and get away with it. Like calling herself a widow. Listening to her going on about men, I don't think there ever was a Mr. Bransby.'

The observation bewildered her visiting relations.

'How can you tell she's never been married?'

'All that talk about female liberation. Maybe she went in for free love. That's what suffragettes believed in those days. I wouldn't be surprised if she was once a single parent herself.'

The antipathy between the women was blatant. For their time together in the conservatory they sat with their backs to one another, never exchanging a word. But the strange and unpredictable resolution to the festering situation came about as a result of Vera Bransby's 100th birthday party. It was organised by the staff and administrators of the residential home. The local press had been invited to photograph and report the gala event. The highlight was to be the presentation of the Queen's telegram of congratulations handed to the centenarian by Mrs. C.-B.'s titled relative and a photograph of her blowing out the 100 candles on the specially baked cake.

For Florence the celebration was a great humiliation. There was no way she could avoid being part of it other than by staying in her room on the pretext of being ill. For the hardy nonagenarian it would merely demonstrate the depth of her spite and pettiness at being outshone by a woman ten years her senior. There had to be another approach and resolution to the dreaded occasion of paper hats and coloured balloons.

To those of the family who knew her well there was the uncharitable thought that it was more than a coincidence that she slipped from her Zimmer frame in full view of the media gathered for the celebratory birthday party. The *Surrey Gazette* published the following day had a photograph of Vera Bransby blowing out the candles on her cake and accepting the Queen's telegram, and by its side a shot of Miss Florence Merryman lying waxlike and unconscious on a stretcher, waiting for an ambulance to take her to Guildford General Hospital.

As far as administrators were concerned, the accident not only temporarily clouded the occasion but secretly filled them with apprehension that if Florence's system did give way to shock and she died the inquest would provide the *Surrey Gazette* with a further item on Lady Beauchamp's residential home for genteel folk, only next time the unplanned publicity would be less than welcome.

But just as the day she fell in Surbiton and lay helpless

blocking her own front door for the second time in months, Florence didn't die from trauma or any other complication. When she returned from hospital several days later with a plaster cast on her arm and trundled into the conservatory in a wheelchair, she felt satisfied with herself for having made a dramatic exit from the hated celebrations and making an equally effective re-entry into the residential home as the centre of attention. However, she was not prepared for the reception that greeted her, which momentarily took her off guard and placed her at a considerable disadvantage.

It was when she'd been wheelchaired to her favourite spot facing the lavender bushes that Vera Bransby got up and turned to face her. When she spoke it was without a trace of bile or sarcasm in her voice.

'You're all right then?'

Florence gave her a withering look and pointed to the plaster cast on her arm.

'All right? Does this look as if it's all right?'

Vera ignored the rebuff. Instead she looked solicitous.

'Shame you missed my party the other day. You'd have enjoyed yourself along with all the others. They made a grand do for me. I even got a telegram from the Queen.'

Florence remained po-faced and unconciliatory.

'I had nothing to celebrate where I was.'

The widow was determined to be friendly.

'There's a picture in the paper. Olivia's lord and me blowing out the candles on the cake. We're all on the front page. You as well.'

Florence hadn't seen the *Surrey Gazette* with a shot of herself lying corpse-like on the conservatory floor.

'I was under sedation. I wasn't allowed newspapers.'

Vera looked genuinely concerned at Florence's catalogue of woe. Suddenly, she pointed to the armchair.

'You can have your seat back if you like.'

The peace offering took Florence by surprise. Her voice was marginally less rancorous than usual.

'Thank you, but I can't get up with my arm in plaster.'

Suddenly, Olivia spoke up for the first time since being displaced in the conservatory and ridiculed in the dining room.

'The Colonel here will give you a hand. Won't you, Colonel?'

He nodded and suddenly the concerted behaviour of her former foes offering friendship and reconciliation was more than Florence Merryman could handle. Her defences began to crumble, even though when she replied her voice still had an edge to it.

'They said at the hospital I was very strong but the next time I fall could be the last time.'

'The Colonel and the nurse will take good care not to drop you.'

It was from that moment of the joint manoeuvre that transferred Florence to her favourite blue-cushioned armchair that peace and harmony prevailed in Lady Beauchamp's home for genteel folk. It was only Florence's visiting family who had to adjust to the changed circumstances of the reconciled quartet. After hearing of Vera Bransby, the Colonel and Olivia C.-B., they raised the question of her volte-face.

'But Aunt Florrie, you said you couldn't stand the sight of these three people, how is it you're now so friendly?'

She looked astonished and affronted by their query.

'Who said I never liked them?'

'You always went on about the widow never having been

married and the toothless woman from Belgrave Square having nothing to be snobbish about. And what about the colonel you threatened to hit with your stick, saying he had no right to be in the convalescent home?'

She was as fierce denying these remarks as she was praising them as bosom companions.

'I don't remember saying awful things about them. Why would I when they're all so nice and friendly to me?'

While the staff were relieved at the prevailing harmony, the administrators were delighted at the prospect of a contented Miss Merryman reaching her centenary with them. It was left to members of the family to calculate the capital required to keep her in the home till then. Though unstated, it was their common thought that it was a very high price to pay for a piece of paper from the reigning monarch in the year 2008.

However, while waiting on events, there was a crumb of comfort for the more socially aware of Florence's family. On regular visits they met up with Olivia's peer, like themselves a dutiful visitor and also a person displaying the greatest solicitude for his residential relation. Occasionally, while Mrs. C.-B. and others cat-napped, he discussed the question of her longevity in objective and philosophical terms.

'Speaking personally, I'm of the view that life has to have a sense of purpose for it to be meaningful. Without purpose it merely becomes existence. The Bible put the span at three score years and ten but there is a case for allowing people to meet their maker at a time of their own choosing. Of course, where euthanasia's concerned there would have to be laws to safeguard the infirm and incapable. You can be sure we in the upper chamber would protect them against the venal knaves of this world.'

It wasn't his title, breeding and charm alone that endeared Mrs. C.-B.'s lord to the family. To those members privileged to hear him hold forth, they were very impressed with the range of his intellectuality. In particular, they found his reference to God very reassuring. It was that and his philosophical attitude to life and death that struck such a chiming chord.

None of Florence's relations had voiced the thought that while summoning help had been the humane thing to do, had the postman not come to their aunt's rescue she might have passed peacefully away in the hallway and had her wish of staying in her Surbiton home to the end granted. In which case, her life would have ended meaningfully instead of continuing an aimless existence as at present in Lady Beauchamp's home for genteel folk in Surrey.

It was only a matter of weeks after her century birthday party and the reconciliation with Florence Merryman that Vera Bransby went to sleep one night after supper and didn't wake up for breakfast. It was almost as if she'd overheard the peer's observation about a purposeless existence and decided that after all she'd lived through, life from now on would be an anti-climax.

As usual, the staff were very discreet and didn't mention her death to the other residents. It was left to a member of Florence's family on a routine visit some days later to observe and query why the widow from Peckham Rye wasn't occupying her usual chair.

'She's probably resting in her room. She is very old.'

Being ten years younger than Vera, Florence didn't regard herself as being very old.

'She was sitting there yesterday. Wasn't she sitting there yesterday, Olivia?'

Mrs. C.-B., besides having no teeth, was also hard of hearing. She smiled and nodded.

'Oh yes, I had lunch yesterday.'

Florence ignored her and turned to the Colonel.

'Wasn't Vera sitting here yesterday?'

The Colonel shrugged indifferently and went on reading.

'Silly old fool. He doesn't know what day it is.'

Mrs. C.-B.'s memory suddenly focused and she beamed.

'I remember. I had lamb. It was very nice.'

Florence was irritated by her forgetfulness, yet still found it necessary to correct her.

'It was beef casserole not lamb.'

'Maybe we'll have lamb today?'

'What's today – Wednesday?'

For the visitor of the day, the conversation took unexpected twists and turns. The question put to them had to be answered.

'No, Aunt Florence – today's Friday.'

'Then it's fish cakes.'

She didn't quibble about the missing days.

'It's always fish cakes on Friday, and bread and butter pudding afterwards.'

Mrs. C.-B. made a wry face.

'Mr. Christie-Bowler would never eat fish cakes. He said they made you fat.'

Florence was sharp and impatient.

'Fish cakes can't make you fat! He meant bread pudding.'

'We had a cook in Belgrave Square.'

'I cooked for myself. I never made fish cakes or bread pudding.'

As they discussed the health aspects of the daily menus, the original query concerning the fate of Vera Bransby was completely forgotten. She might come down for lunch or she might stay in her room. Either way, she didn't interfere with their routine.

For Florence's relatives, the burden of duty visits was passing the time and finding something to say. Ever-present in their minds were the same questions – how long her money would last, and if it ran out, how much it would cost to keep her there in Surrey or a home that didn't cater for retired genteel folk. They were all caring, dutiful and altruistic and never voiced such selfish and mercenary thoughts. The even more intriguing and unexpressed enigma was that if she did die while still in credit, who among them would benefit most?

But none predicted the answers to the conundrums. When one summer's day they found Aunt Florence lying in the garden it was assumed she'd toppled over while bending down to smell the lavender bushes. On the face of it, the prediction that the third time she fell might be the last proved to be accurate, but the post-mortem revealed it wasn't the fall that killed her, it was a bee's sting that paralysed her nervous system and caused her heart to stop. It was ironic but fitting for her to die lying crumpled among the bushes she often sat by and admired because they were her favourite colour of blue.

When the funeral was over and the contents of her will made known, it was the turn of the members of the family to receive a shock to their systems. As rewards for consigning her to a convalescent home conveniently near to their various homes instead of keeping her in her own flat, she decided against leaving her wealth and possessions to any of them. The only consolation left was that her death had spared them the financial burden of keeping her at Lady Beauchamp's residential home for genteel folk in Surrey.

At the end of the day, the waspish obstinate spinster who forgot to wear the lanyard round her neck and as a result lay helpless in the hall blocking her own front door, left her remaining capital of £500 and the blue Persian rug to the dogs home in Battersea. When it came to the moment of truth for all the members of her large and solicitous family, Aunt Florrie had finally blown the whistle on them all.

ODYSSEY OF THE AMMONATIS

The summer sun gleamed on the surface of the river at Richmond-upon-Thames. It warmed the wooden deck of the long sleek yacht towering above the collection of cabin cruisers, sailing dinghies, rowing boats and flat-bottomed punts, their occupants curious to know why a 140ft ocean-going craft was waiting to enter the lock gates, and like themselves, journey upstream to narrower waters. Their interest was shared by a cluster of people gathered along the towpath, including a local reporter with a box camera, for on that sunny afternoon in July 1939, the *Ammonatis* was a sight to behold. I know, for I was standing on the largest vessel ever to have sailed westwards from London Bridge.

As a 21-year-old university student during midterm vacation I'd volunteered to be an unpaid crewman for the journey from the Thames Estuary at Southend-on-Sea to a berth at Walton-on-Thames where the vessel's owner lived. All I knew about the *Ammonatis* was that the slender graceful boat had once been part of the German Navy and harried English submarines during 1914–18 – not that it bore a Greek-sounding name with the myths of Poseidon and Neptune during those years of war. That was the brainchild of the owner who converted it into a pleasure cruiser fit to journey any of the world's waterways. On that afternoon in July 1939, no one could predict the vessel's final voyage nor the effect it would play on several people's lives. It was only in retrospect it occurred to me that if the small destroyer had been left moth-balled in a Hamburg shipyard till the Second World War, it might have been used for a second time chasing and sinking British submarines. Instead the role of this refashioned ship was to be dramatically reversed and in the process make something of a saga out of the events that followed this journey from Southend-on-Sea to Walton-on-Thames.

In my virgin nautical experience, the skipper of the *Ammonatis* was an impressive figure who could have graced the bridge of an ocean liner and for all I knew may have done so in his career. It was impossible for me to judge his age because his face was covered with a beard I'd only seen on a packet of John Player's cigarettes. But to complete the impressive appearance he wore a naval cap, reefer jacket and black trousers. Only his canvas plimsolls spoiled the overall effect.

I watched as he leapt from the rail onto the towpath and walked towards the lock keeper who unlike the rest of the onlookers was viewing the *Ammonatis* with a doubtful expression and shaking his head from side to side. I had no more knowledge of England's inland rivers than I had of the open sea but it was obvious the man was uncertain whether the vessel would fit into the lock, and even if it did, what damage it might do in the process. As befitted an ex-naval commander, the skipper assured him that not only was there room for the yacht to enter the lock and continue its journey upstream but several other craft could cram in without harm. He then vaulted back on board and took up his position behind the wheel in the small bridge house. True to type and tradition of the strong silent sailor, he nodded for me to untie the mooring ropes fore and aft, started the diesel engine and inched the vessel through the open gates. It was then that I understood the keeper's concern. Though there was room to spare lengthways, across the width of the lock it was tight, and the few rowing boats and punts that manoeuvred to our side were tight up against the stone wall. As for my duties during the process, all I had to do was watch the fenders placed there to stop any damage to our painted sides – not that I could have done anything had they broken free and the rough surface scraped and scored our immaculate hull as the water raised us to the required level.

After a few minutes the lock gates opened and we steered out to midstream. I was surprised when people on the bank cheered and clapped. I felt it inappropriate to wave back so left it to the navigator to acknowledge their appreciation, which he did by saluting in naval fashion. From then on our journey was uneventful because news of our approach was relayed via Richmond to the keepers at Teddington, Moseley and Sunbury, and the captain had no need to convince them that despite its massive appearance there was room enough for *Ammonatis* to negotiate in and out of their locks.

It was several hours before we came alongside the owner's home at Walton. The house was fronted by a lawn that led to the river's edge and the yacht extended the width of it fore and aft. With the engine cut and anchor dropped, the skipper slung a small ladder over the side and with two large spikes and heavy hammer in his hands stepped onto the grass. He pounded one into the turf one side of the lush lawn and the second metal peg into the other. He then called for me to throw ropes coiled on deck and tied them round the makeshift bollards. When he was satisfied the vessel was safely secured he came back on board, and taking a stool from the wheelhouse, sat down, filled and lit a pipe, and relaxed.

All this was done with hardly a word spoken between us. It was early evening and the sun was still bright and warm.

There were cabin cruisers and sailing dinghies travelling up and down stream, some gliding with the current and others struggling against it. Several empty boats were moored alongside a riverside pub. It was a peaceful, idyllic summer scene.

In all the time we'd been together since I joined him at Southend, except for introducing himself as Jamie MacDougal and asking me my name, we'd hardly spoken. The item in the university house magazine asked for an unpaid volunteer to help crew a boat up the River Thames. It didn't say what the programme was once we reached Walton. It seemed to me that whoever placed the ad was looking for someone with a taste for adventure and I considered I fitted the bill. As a schoolboy I'd been an army cadet and now, at 20 years of age in July 1939, was a lance corporal in the Territorial Army. As I sat watching him puffing away I was convinced it was the taciturn Scot himself who'd placed the ad. Suddenly, he took me by surprise.

'Where you from, lad?'

'East London. Canning Town.'

'Know the river then?'

'As far as the docks in the Isle of Dogs. I see ships there from all over the world. As a youngster I always wanted to be on one going to some far-off place.'

'Why didn't you?'

Thinking back now, his remark was reasonable. I'd volunteered for an adventure on the river in a small boat – why hadn't I sailed the oceans on a large one? I didn't want to go into detail and mention my humble background with a father who worked as a loader in the East India Docks and a mother who did office cleaning so that I could stay on at school until my 16th birthday. In 1937, winning a scholarship and going on to higher education was one way out of London's East End slums. I shrugged and turned his question instead.

'Have you sailed round the world?'

'You name it, laddie – I've been there.'

He didn't elaborate and I sat conjuring images of romantic places I'd only seen in geographical magazines and cinemas. He puffed silently for several minutes, then knocking his pipe on the rail, pointed to the pub across the river.

'Let's have a drink in the Anglers Arms. We've earned it.'

I judged the width of the river to be about 50 yards and wondered if he meant we should strip and swim across. Instead of waiting for an answer he walked to the stern and unlashed a small dinghy tied to the deck. He lowered it into the water and waited for me to clamber in. It only took him a few strong pulls on the oars to reach the other side and tie up at the bank in front of the riverside pub. Inside there were a number of people and they greeted us as if we were naval celebrities. It was obvious our arrival had made a profound impression on the river-goers of Walton-on-Thames. When the thumping and applause had died down, the landlord, who was drawing ale behind the bar, spoke for them all.

'Looking at it from here she seems as big as the *Queen Mary*! Billy-boy West ought to have been here to run up a flag – or fire a cannon.'

It was plain the landlord was referring to the owner of the magnificent riverside home as well as the luxurious yacht now moored in front of it.

'We guessed he was well-heeled but that must have cost him a bob or two!'

With that scarcely veiled envious reference to the absent owner over and done with, the customers' attention focused on the bearded captain. In the fulsome comments and smiles of approval that followed, it was clear Jamie MacDougal from Clydeside Glasgow was regarded by all the locals as someone special. So much so that not once during the time we spent at the bar did he pay for a round. My glass too was kept topped up, with the result that before long, my head, bladder and stomach were giving me trouble. It was ten o'clock when the landlord called time and everyone left the Anglers Arms and dispersed into the night. I had no idea what was going to happen next; whether I was expected to make my way back to London as best I could or find a sheltered spot along the riverbank and complete the day's adventure by sleeping rough. It was the bearded skipper himself who took me completely by surprise.

'Come on, laddie. It's time for grub!'

With that he stepped into the dinghy, and barely giving me time to scramble in, pulled across the dark water to the far bank. Without a word he tied up and climbed aboard. He then went below to a small galley and set about frying eggs and bacon. It was obvious he was as expert preparing food in *Ammonatis*'s tiny kitchen as he was at the wheel piloting her safely from Southend-on-Sea to Walton-on-Thames.

When we'd both finished eating he nodded to our empty plates.

'Clear away before coming up. Keep things shipshape.'

It was an order. He was the captain and I the cabin boy. When I'd washed up and put everything away I joined him on deck, puffing away at his pipe and staring up at the stars. He was a picture of physical and mental contentment. For my part, I was still uncertain about the future. It was nearing midnight and though well past my normal bedtime I didn't want to give the impression I was overly concerned at the lateness of the hour. I made my voice sound as casual as I knew how.

'I didn't reckon on staying on *Ammonatis* overnight.'

He kept the pipe clenched between his teeth.

'You aiming to walk to the Isle of Dogs?'

I wasn't sure if he was being sarcastic. I was immediately on the defensive.

'I could if I had to. I've done 20-mile hikes with the territorials.'

He walked over to the small wheelhouse and tapped the barometer.

'The glass is set fair. Walton's not a bad place to be moored. The owner's not due till Saturday. You could stay till then if you want.'

From first thing that morning I'd found everything about Jamie MacDougal different from anyone I ever knew, but nothing surprised me more than his unexpected invitation to holiday on *Ammonatis* for the rest of the week. Untypically, I found myself aping him and replying in a clipped tone and minimum words.

'Thanks! I'll nip home in the morning and pack some things.'

He didn't bother to nod.

'Bring a bottle back with you.'

That was the end of our conversation. Sitting on deck listening to the muted sound of water tumbling over an upstream weir I revelled in the peaceful atmosphere. From the day's early start at Southend, through the crowded pool of London and on to Walton-on-Thames, everything had gone smoothly, and now I had the rest of the week in circumstances as far removed from drab Canning Town as it was possible to be. Life for me that warm summer night in July 1939 was very sweet indeed.

After a while, Jamie tapped the dottle from his pipe and without a word led the way below, closing and securing a small hatch above his head.

'Keep out the rats!'

He didn't bother to say goodnight before entering a cabin and leaving me to choose my own berth. I lay down on the lower of a two-tier bunk and for the first time since stepping aboard *Ammonatis* was aware of the sound of water lapping against its hull and the gentle swaying motion as it pulled against the rope stays. In the long silent night that followed I twisted and turned restlessly, whereas at home in noisy Canning Town I slept like a log.

The following morning I caught the first train to London. At home I packed some clothes and a pair of swimming trunks and with a silent nod from my mother took the half bottle of Scotch my father kept for what he termed 'medicinal purposes'. I was back aboard *Ammonatis* by noon and spent the next five days polishing brass fitments on deck and wiping the diesel engine below. In between I shopped for food and at the chandlers for bits and bobs. In effect I was Jamie MacDougal's dogsbody and I enjoyed every single moment of it.

Mid-week a newspaper reporter rowed across from the Anglers and came aboard. After talking to the skipper about its history since its conversion from a German Navy submarine chaser to a luxury yacht he asked me to dive from the ship's rail into the river. He said a photograph would add a human dimension to the story. The following day it was published in a national daily and though *Ammonatis* dominated the top of the page and the write-up referred to Jamie MacDougal as a typical man of the sea, there was no mention of my name. I didn't keep a copy of the issue. In July 1939, I had no sense of its historical interest. Besides which, the shot of my ugly belly flop was nothing to write home about.

It was the arrival of the yacht's owner with his family a day earlier than expected that changed everything for me that week – and the future too. When I first caught sight of Mr. William West I understood why the landlord of the Anglers Arms referred to his cross-river neighbour as Billy-boy. He was short and round and walked stiff-legged, rather like a clockwork toy. Poor as a church mouse or rich as Croesus, the publican's nickname suited him to perfection.

He was surprised to find me aboard but when Jamie MacDougal told him it was as a reward for helping to skipper *Ammonatis* from Southend to Walton as an unpaid deckhand he became very complimentary.

'Jolly good of you to help out, young man. What's your name?'

'Leonard. Leonard Patterson.'

'What do you do, Lennie? What's your job?'

'I'm studying for a degree.'

'Is that a fact? A university student! Your folks are well-off then?'

It was more a statement than a question. I felt embarrassed to talk of my background.

'I won a scholarship. I've got a grant from the council.'

He was impressed and nodded approvingly.

'Good for you! Doing things the hard way. You must tell my family about it. Come and have tea with us – that's if the skipper can spare you.'

He kept a straight face as if acknowledging Jamie MacDougal's maritime right to invite a stranger on board and holiday at his employer's expense. For his part, the bearded captain went along with the charade.

'So long as things are shipshape he can go when his dogwatch is done. Four bells sharp.'

And so the fateful social meeting took place as arranged. When I left the yacht and started walking up to the house I was met by a skinny youth and a few steps behind him a winsome girl several years older. From their father's reference to youngsters, I'd imagined his offspring to be two high-spirited infants but they were as different from that mental image as it was possible to be. Most intimate and lasting relationships are forged from first impressions and on that summer afternoon in July 1939, coming face to face as we did, the three of us were no exceptions to the rule. For absolutely no reason but to justify his excited reaction, young Royston West looked upon me as a bold adventurer who'd braved the elements to help bring *Ammonatis* up the River Thames. As for his sister Avril, when our eyes met we were already passionately in love, even before we had sat down at her parents' table for tea. It was an acute attack of love at first sight and the world was a different place from that moment on.

At the tea table, Mr. West was as tolerant and jolly with his wife and children as he had been earlier on with Jamie MacDougal and me. He seemed to look for and find the congenial side of everything and the best in everybody. Mrs. West too was good-natured and motherly and within minutes treated me as if I'd been an intimate of the West family all my life. I felt completely at home and where I naturally belonged despite my humble background. And almost as if he was determined to make an enjoyable situation even more so, at a well-chosen moment in the conversation, Mr. Billy-boy West made a surprise announcement.

'You said it's end of term at university. Why not stay here till the next one starts? The skipper wouldn't object. Neither would Royston and Avril, that's for sure.'

There were wildly excited nods from both while Mrs. West went even further to endorse her husband's open-handed invitation.

'You don't have to sleep on a bunk in the boat, either. We've room in the house and one more for breakfast won't matter.'

The excitement was too much for Royston who whooped for joy and rattled his spoon against a teacup while Avril looked at me with lovesick eyes, silently beseeching me to accept. It was going against nature not to. Even had I been otherwise committed I'd have broken any arrangement. And so it came about that during the remainder of July, the whole of August, and part of September 1939, I stayed at Walton-on-Thames in a state of physical and emotional euphoria, a condition that in a lifetime since I've never once recaptured. And then, as if my idyllic existence wasn't pleasure enough, one day as we all sat sunbathing on *Ammonatis*, there came a statement from Mr. West that capped it all.

'Mrs. West and I usually go abroad in winter. That's why I bought *Ammonatis*. How'd you like to come along as Jamie's mate? You never know, when it's nice and safe somewhere in the Mediterranean, he might even let you take the wheel.'

The invitation into a dream world touring the world's playground was put in the offhand manner of a man who regarded his sybaritic lifestyle as natural as breathing air. I was stunned mute. The nearest I'd ever been to an ocean was Southend-on-Sea – an East Londoner's holiday Mecca with its night-time illuminations strung along the promenade and air smelling of Thames Estuary ozone and fried onions. The magical names of Cannes, Nice, Genoa and Naples one side of the Mediterranean and Tunis on the other were mind-bending fantasies. They were the far and away places I had dreamed of as I lay in my bed at night listening to ships fog-horning in and out of East India docks. It was several seconds before I had control of my senses.

'How long would we be away?'

'Come back in the spring – March or April maybe.'

A six-month vacation cruising the French and Italian Rivieras was beyond my wildest imagination. All thoughts of a university degree and its opportunity to escape the drudgery of a humdrum career were swamped by the magnificent offer, and as if all his beneficence was not enough, he made my final decision easier still.

'If you're worried about losing your scholarship grant I can take care of that when we come back. It can't cost a fortune to get a degree.'

There were heart-rending looks from Avril, and Royston balancing on the ship's rail nodded so vigorously he almost fell off it into the river. Even Mrs. West added her sentiments to their silent appeals.

'Your parents wouldn't mind you spending Christmas with us, would they?'

And so it was agreed that instead of spending the winter of 1939 shrouded by London's leaden skies and foggy air, it would be spent cruising the Mediterranean under azure skies and warm sunshine. The future for me had everything to offer. At 20 years of age, being in seventh heaven was a living reality.

Whether it was because of his disinterest in politics or disbelief there could be another war so soon after the end of the last, Mr. West's holiday plans for the winter of 1939 took no account of Hitler's objectives covering the same period. On the other hand, Jamie had a decided view of the Führer and his global intentions.

'Wouldn't trust the bugger further than I can spit! We should have done something about him when he marched into the Rhineland.'

When that reoccupation took place in May 1936 I didn't have a political thought in my head, and in spite of being a territorial soldier sworn to defend King and Country, in August 1939 I was still indifferent as to what was going on in Europe. But to me the *Ammonatis*'s skipper was a profound thinker on the subject and I listened to everything he had to say.

'I know the Hun! Arrogant when he's up and cringing when he's down. Thought he had us beat in 1918 with their blockade and very nearly had! Now they're saying they never really lost the war.'

His reference to the knife-edge outcome of the Great War impressed me greatly. I imagined him as a fearless naval captain engaging German battleships in desperate attempts to break their stranglehold on our vital supply routes which threatened ignominious defeat. Just as I appeared heroic to young Royston West in September 1939, the bearded skipper was a real-life hero to me.

Regardless of what was going on in the rest of the world, in early autumn with the days still bright and warm we were all enjoying ourselves at Walton-on-Thames. One day aboard *Ammonatis*, Royston and I were taking turns diving from its rail into the river – he to impress me and I to swank to Avril and her parents as they looked on with pride and pleasure. As usual when his employer was aboard, Jamie MacDougal found things that needed servicing in the engine, even though the vessel hadn't moved a yard since we moored more than two months before.

It was Mrs. West who first noticed the man on the far bank standing outside the Anglers Arms. At first she assumed he was waving at *Ammonatis*, expressing appreciation at the sight of us all enjoying ourselves on the resplendent boat. It was only when he persisted in attracting our attention and she commented on the funny little man who must have had too much to drink in the public house that I glanced across and recognised my father. At that unexpectedly critical moment in my life I didn't think it appropriate to inform them the funny little man who might have had too much to drink in the Anglers Arms was a docker from Canning Town and that day in Walton wasn't quite the time or place to hob-knob with the wealthy Wests. It was snobbery that motivated me to plunge into the river and swim across to him. He held out an envelope he'd been holding and waving to attract our attention.

'This came for you first post. I thought you ought to see it.'

The note inside was brief. I was to report to battalion headquarters immediately. It was at that moment, glancing from the military summons in my dripping hand to the happy family gathered on *Ammonatis*, that I sensed the party was over. Perhaps my father read my mind, as he patted me on the shoulder in a rare gesture of affection.

'Sorry to break up your party, Lennie. I'll see you back home.'

With that he waved to the Wests, turned and walked off. It was as if he too felt it inappropriate for him to intrude on my new friends. I waited till he was out of sight, folded the note and gripped it between my teeth, then swam back to the boat.

When I explained who it was who'd waved at us, Mr. West expressed sincere disappointment that I hadn't invited him to meet the family.

'I'd have liked to talk to your father. He must be an interesting man.'

Mrs. West was even more dismayed.

'What must he have thought of us coming all the way from London and not being asked across for a cup of tea?'

There were even greater reactions of regret to the news that I was to report to barracks immediately. Royston fell silent and glum while Avril choked on tears as she asked how long I'd be away. I shrugged, attempting to hide my sadness at having to leave her and the family and even being optimistic about the future.

'It may only be manoeuvres. A couple of weeks maybe.'

It was Jamie MacDougal who put it on the line for everyone.

'That bit of paper means the Government's expecting trouble. Things are hotting up with Hitler. We're in for another war with Germany. It's mobilisation time!'

Mr. West regarded his interpretation of the political scene as far-fetched and alarmist and was unusually sharp-toned in replying to the gloomy forecast.

'Lennie says it's probably manoeuvres and soldiers have to keep in practice, even part-time territorials. There's no point reading more into it than that.'

Despite his attempt at lightening the mood, from then on the atmosphere changed. Suddenly, everything around me looked the same yet was indefinably different. It was as if my summons to report for duty was a foreboding of dramatic times to come, though not even the *Ammonatis*'s far-seeing skipper could anticipate that on that summer afternoon in 1939 we were only three days away from being at war with Hitler's Germany, and that as a result of it none of our individual lives would ever be the same again.

As I thanked Mr. and Mrs. West for their hospitality, saying I hoped to see them soon, young Royston showed his feelings by angrily throwing stones into the river while Avril, inconsolable at my departure, rushed weeping to the house, unable to face a lovers' farewell. Jamie MacDougal sat in the dinghy waiting while I packed my things and as he rowed me across the river I was convinced I'd never see any of them again. When we reached the bank fronting the Anglers Arms he followed me out onto the towpath.

'One for the road, Lennie boy, and a long one it's going to be!'

We'd spent each day of the past two months together and in spite of the differences in our ages, temperaments and experiences had formed a close bond. Inside the pub he looked back to the *Ammonatis* and raised his glass.

'Pity she's too old for service. Just like me.'

When it came to the moment of saying goodbye it was no surprise to me that he stayed in character and without a hint of sentimentality switched the conversation.

'You forgot your swimming trunks. They're on the engine drying out.'

In the weeks of our association I'd acquired his habit of speaking tersely.

'Keep them till I come back.'

'I'll see the moths don't get at them.'

He downed his whisky and glanced up at the clock above the bar.

'You'd best be making for the train.'

With that he waved to the landlord and walked to the dinghy. I didn't wait for him to be facing me as he rowed back to the yacht. Instead I turned my back and strode away from what had been the most magical interlude of my young life.

It was two days later, Sunday the 3rd of September, that I listened to Prime Minister Neville Chamberlain's thin, tremulous voice announcing the start of the Second World War.

From that announcement onwards, except for the sounding of an air raid alarm and instantaneous all-clear, there was nothing exciting about the day. In spite of a state of war existing between Great Britain and Germany, our commanding officer and adjutant inspected us with the same gimlet eyes as on any of our pre-war evening assemblies. If we were prepared to die for King and Country, our brasses and toe caps had to be immaculate. The Wehrmacht might produce fearsome warriors on the battlefield but the British Army were unsurpassed on ceremonial parade.

***

The end of 1939 and beginning of 1940 was spent guarding a gasworks in Essex which in military jargon was referred to as a VP. I was familiar with the installation which was near to Canning Town, though it never occurred to me that one day me and my platoon would be watching out for German parachutists to land and destroy it and win the war for Hitler. Then, without a moment's notice, we were transferred to a hush-hush headquarters in Uxbridge which was so secret we weren't supposed to refer to it even among ourselves. The boring routine continued throughout the bitterly cold months of January, February and March, and then in April, when we'd made everything cosy in the guard hut and were enjoying intimate relations with the WAAFs on duty inside the secret establishment, without a moment's notice we were bussed onto a fleet of charabancs and driven to Seaford Harbour in Sussex. There we assembled with the rest of the battalion and crammed into every available space on a cross-channel ferry sailed to the Belgian port of Zeebrugge.

Going abroad for the first time in my life was not at all the exciting experience I'd dreamed about in Walton-on-Thames. The overloaded vessel made heavy weather of the crossing. At the end of a bilious five hours we were dumped on the foreshore between the port and Ostend and left to fend for ourselves. For the first few days it seemed no one knew we were coming, and just as nature abhors a vacuum, rumours circulated in the place of official information. We were going to march through the gap between the French Army in their Maginot Line and attack the Germans on their exposed flank. Then we'd march to Berlin and hoist the Union Jack over the Reichstag and the war would be over. That communiqué lasted several hours. Then it appeared Hitler had taken such fright at the sight of the British Army landing in Belgium he'd waved the white flag. The only reason we were still on the outskirts of Zeebrugge was because we were waiting for a ferry to take us back to England. Then came the definitive explanation. The phoney war was only phoney in the sense that no one actually wanted to fight another one. As a result, the leaders of Britain, Germany and France had talked it over and decided everyone should go home and forget about the Second World War.

It was when we were ordered to pack up and march inland that a final definitive rumour took root. It was obvious that as the most well-trained and efficient unit in the entire BEF we were being moved to the front to prevent Hitler's army breaking through to the coast. At that juncture, optimism gave way to reality. As everyone in my platoon knew, the only armoured vehicle our company possessed was a Bren Carrier, and even though it clattered on tracks just like a tank, when it came right down to it was no match for a German Panzer.

In fact, we never met the feared and fearsome opposition. Marching in full pack with only five-minute breaks each hour, the battalion was diverted from its original course south towards the front and was now heading east into France.

Late that afternoon we marched into another Belgian coastal resort, Dunkirk. It was too cloudy to see the white cliffs of Dover and the Channel didn't seem much different to being on the seafront in the South of England. Our platoon was allotted a barn in an orchard on the outskirts of the town. As a billet it was a great improvement on Ostend's gritty beach, and after a tiring day was a very welcome relief, even though we were ordered to remain in full kit and take up defensive positions. My years as a territorial soldier had conditioned me to look at fields and woodlands from a military perspective. It had been dinned into me by instructors taking their military wisdom from peacetime training manuals. Camouflaged positions for machine guns, slit trenches to shelter from mortars, fields of fire for riflemen, and line of retreat if and when things went wrong.

As to that last eventuality, it required little military expertise and less imagination on our part to realise that the platoon's line of retreat led straight into the sea. That was for officers to worry about as they attended briefings at battalion HQ. There was an unshakeable element of faith by TA rankers in men who held HM commissions. To us they were knowledgeable, authoritative and fearless. We never came into contact with staff officers who wore red bands round their caps but we were confident they too could be relied on to deal with any and every military situation. There was no reason for us to modify those opinions, not until an increasing mass of troops packed into the Dunkirk area between April and May 1940 and it dawned on the least imaginative squaddie that what was happening to the BEF was not, in military terms, a tactical retreat – it was a rout.

Not that there was a sense of gloom at the prospect, at least not until the Luftwaffe appeared and without a Spitfire or Hurricane to harry them gave us our first taste of the nastiness of war. Like the well-drilled soldiers we were supposed to be, we put our training into effect. When enemy planes appeared we huddled in slit trenches with our heads below ground. Not that we were cowardly or inefficient soldiers during those attacks, but the fact remains that had the enemy suddenly appeared and advanced towards us they'd have met with limited opposition. In fact, Dunkirk was nothing like VP duty at Beckton Gas Works or the RAF establishment at Uxbridge. It wasn't a handful of Germans dropping from the sky we had to watch for, it was an army of Huns who could be as close as the poplar trees the far side of the field.

Fortunately for us, that situation didn't arise, and when the long night was over and skies lightened, the waters in and around the port of Dunkirk were filled with vessels of every description. There were yachts, sloops, ketches, cabin cruisers, motorboats and tugs, and further out between naval frigates and destroyers there were ferries, coastal lighters and paddle steamers. As a spectacle it outshone any painting of historic battles. Neither Nelson at Trafalgar nor Drake at Plymouth could have witnessed such an armada of craft.

In the years that have passed since that fateful occasion,

romantics have come to regard the retreat as an epic adventure, but there was nothing epic or adventurous to soldiers wading waist-high in the sea with rifles held above their heads and making for vessels with room to take them aboard while Messerschmidts and Heinkels strafed and bombed them every inch of the way. As my platoon lined up to enter the sea, military discipline prevailed to the edge of the beach, but 50 yards later, individually hauled dripping wet onto tiny boats, the experience was incompatible with military heroics. During the time I was in the water my equipment came adrift and I crossed the Channel minus a helmet, trousers and a boot. It was on a Yarmouth trawler which with its rolling action and smell of fish was a far more unpleasant experience than the crowded ferry from Seaford to Zeebrugge a few weeks before.

***

After the war I decided to ignore old wives' warnings about revisiting places of past pleasures and decided to go to Walton-on-Thames. There was no question of my looking to rekindle a long-lost romance with Avril West. I'd long since married the WAAF I'd fallen in love with when I was at Bomber Command's secret establishment in Uxbridge in 1940.

At the time of my revisit to Walton-on-Thames I had my wife and two young children with me. As we drove to the riverside town I reflected that at 32 years of age I was as different from the downy-faced youth of 1939 as it was possible to be and secretly apprehensive as to how the family would react to me. For my part, I imagined they and everything around them would be exactly the same. Jolly roly-poly Billy-boy West and motherly, matronly Mrs. West. Doe-eyed Avril and devoted Royston. The *Ammonatis* with Jamie MacDougal aboard admired by river-goers in punts and rowboats and the house with its weedless lawn reaching the water's edge. The whole idyllic setting was etched into my memory like an engraved print. There'd been no Blitz on Walton as there'd been on Canning Town. Nothing there could have been or would have been affected by the war. I was hoping that this visit would be the one occasion when old wives' tales and wiseacres' warnings would be proved totally and utterly wrong.

There was no question of driving to the Anglers Arms and waving across the river to attract the Wests' attention as my father had done when he came to bring me my calling-up paper in 1939. Nor ferrying across river in a rowboat and making a surprise appearance on the West's sloping lush lawn. Instead I drove over Walton Bridge to the rear of the house and parked a little way from the entrance, feeling it tactful to appear alone than en famille.

When Royston West opened the door there was a split second when neither of us recognised the other. In place of the scrawny 14-year-old schoolboy there stood a sturdy man who topped me by several inches. Then the shock of surprise wore off and he grasped my hand and wrung it enthusiastically. He glanced over my shoulder to the car and beckoned to my wife and with our children led us all through the house to the riverside garden. There was a young woman sitting in a deck chair holding the rein of a harness attached to a toddler crawling around on the Cumberland turf. She looked puzzled till Royston explained who we were, then broke into a cheerful welcoming smile. Within seconds she and my wife were in deep and intimate conversation; so much so that our older children were instructed to act as loco parentis to the energetically adventurous child and take charge of the toddler rein. Thus

Royston and I were able to leave them, and sitting close to the water's edge, reminisce about the blissful summer of 1939.

Without needing to close my eyes to recapture past images, I was in a time warp. Looking up and down river then across to the Anglers Arms, everything was exactly the same. I could hear the water rushing over the upstream weir and as I watched punts and rowboats maneuvering to avoid bankside washes created by motorboats I thought of Jamie MacDougal viewing them from the deck of *Ammonatis* and his scathing views of inconsiderate sailors. I was back in time when the world was a joyful place and nothing yet had happened in life to spoil it for me. Only the squeals of my children as they played with their real-life toy broke the spell to remind me that though things looked the same, they were not.

In the years that had passed since we last saw each other, Royston West had changed greatly. He was no longer the gawky lad who'd followed me around like a shadow. The differences between us were as nothing compared to the 14-year-old schoolboy for his hero of legal manhood. There was a note of seriousness in his voice when he asked what had happened to me since I left Walton and returned to London and mobilisation. It took me little more than a minute to span the years since we last met. I spoke truthfully when I said I'd done nothing more than other servicemen called to arms and was thankful to have survived the war all in one piece. I gained the impression that he read more into my honest account simply because it didn't square with the man he'd idolised as a boy. I was his hero and ipso facto between the beginning and end of the Second World War must have done something heroic. For my part, I was keener to hear about the West family since August 1939 and he was swift to oblige.

'I was at school till 18, then deferred call-up till I graduated from Cambridge. I did National Service in 1947. Because I'd been to university I was given a pip and posted to the Army Education Corps. For the most part I taught illiterate soldiers to read and write. I never got further than Bulford Camp in Wiltshire. It wasn't very exciting.'

I felt guilty at the thought but was relieved he'd done nothing exceptional. I would have found it hard if our roles had been reversed and he'd excelled himself as a commissioned officer. I was glad the personal details were over and done with.

'How are your parents keeping?'

'Mum and Dad? Older, but just the same.'

'And Avril?'

Unaccountably, my pulse beat faster, but the excitement was short-lived.

'Avril's fine. She's married and lives in Kent. I'm Uncle Roy – twice over!'

'As a matter of fact, she's with my folks right now in Gibraltar.'

'They're going on from there to the French and Italian Rivieras. Gail and I didn't go with them because she's expecting. Besides, she gets seasick on a boat even when its moored to the bank.'

I tried not to sound wistful for the past nor envious for the present.

'It's taken your dad a long time, but he's made it in the end.'

'If *Ammonatis* had been ready he'd have gone the day war ended.'

At last I had the chance to ask about the other person who was really uppermost in my mind – skipper Jamie MacDougal.

'The yacht was still in mothballs?'

'Not in mothballs. In dry dock at Shoeburyness.'

I racked my brains but couldn't think why *Ammonatis* would be even further down the Thames Estuary than in July 1939 when it had taken Jamie MacDougal and myself all those hours to bring her to Walton.

'In dry dock at Shoeburyness?'

'That's where she was salvaged.'

There was no logic to it but for the first time since I arrived, it was as if a puff of cloud had unexpectedly flitted across the Sun and cast a shadow over the scene.

'Salvaged?'

'It's where *Ammonatis* sank, a mile or so offshore in May 1940.'

I stared at him, bewildered and speechless. It seemed as if he too was determined to be unemotional detailing a highly dramatic event of the Second World War.

'When Dad was asked if she could help evacuate the army at Dunkirk he said it seemed as if fate had stepped in and arranged for the old German submarine-chaser to do war duty for England this time round. Jamie MacDougal was more than willing. He'd already said he was about to leave and sign on in the navy.'

With mention of his name, a mental image flashed before me. I saw him on the bridge of a warship, the personification of a brave seaman facing dangers from above, on and below the surface of the sea, and meeting them all without a quiver of emotion or fear. He was the man I most admired and the idealised memory of him had never dimmed.

'Dad and I went on her as far as London. We stood on Tower Bridge and watched as she sailed downstream. Jamie waved and gave a toot on the horn. I remember thinking how tiny *Ammonatis* looked compared to the ships tied up either side of the river. I really couldn't see it being much use to the army.'

It was a strange feeling listening to the grown man giving his boyhood recollection of an historic event.

'Of course, Dad didn't hear what happened to her right away.'

'What happened to her?'

'That's where she'd gone down.'

I stared at him wide-eyed and speechless.

'They said the bottom of the boat looked as if it had hit a mine and it must have sunk like a stone. They made no mention of a body being in the wreck. You can imagine how the news hit us that Jamie had probably been blown to bits.'

I sat sad and silent, wondering about the coincidental circumstances that in one instance claimed my boyhood idol Jamie MacDougal on his way to rescue troops at Dunkirk and my own ungallant scramble to safety aboard a Yarmouth trawler from the same beleaguered beaches. I was thankful not to have mentioned the incident earlier on.

'There was no question of *Ammonatis* being repaired and brought back right away. It had to be decided who was responsible for it being lost. As a result, she spent the war on a cradle in the boatshed before she was refitted and returned to Walton earlier this year.'

My thoughts immediately went back to July 1939 when I helped bring the yacht upstream through the locks at Richmond, Teddington, Molesey and Sunbury. It was yet another time warp back to that gloriously happy time. Royston seemed to read my mind.

'Dad didn't have to advertise for a student to bring her

up the estuary this time. Besides myself, there was Avril's husband. She'd married him when she was a Wren in 1943 and he was on minesweepers.'

The mention of her name jolted me back to the present. I had a sudden vision of her radiant in glamorous naval uniform and even more attractive than the doe-eyed, soft-cheeked sweetheart of my youth.

'He's with her now on *Ammonatis* doing the Mediterranean trip.'

Somehow the fact of Avril West having a husband qualified to navigate *Ammonatis* deepened my feelings of loss. It was as if a usurper had been put in charge of the vessel of my dreams and ended all my cherished memories of Jamie MacDougal. At that moment I silently wished the boat had remained in its watery graveyard off Shoeburyness and never sailed again. Suddenly, Royston's voice changed and he was his cheerful bouncy self again.

'Not that he'll ever get his hands on the wheel. As the skipper said before he left, ten years was a long time to get to the Med but everything comes to him who waits. I reckon the bearded wonder will sail *Ammonatis* every knot of the way.'

I suppose I must have looked comical, dumbfounded and with staring eyes, and it was at that moment I suspected Royston had deliberately left the most important part of his story to the last moment to produce the greatest dramatic effect.

'You assumed Jamie bought it when *Ammonatis* went down, just as we did?'

Unaccountably, I felt put out by the deception and struggled to keep my feelings from showing and an accusative tone from my voice.

'You said the shipyard thought it hit a mine.'

'We didn't hear what actually happened for more than a year. It seemed the explosion blew him into the water and he was picked up by a passing boat. Besides most of his bones being broken he suffered a complete loss of memory and without any identity on him when he was picked up no one knew who to contact to say he was still alive. The amnesia lasted till 1941 and when he recovered he phoned Dad from hospital to say he was discharged as fit. As there was nothing for him at Walton he got a job in the docks at Chatham and stayed there till the war was over. It went without saying as soon as he heard *Ammonatis* was seaworthy the old skipper was back on board.'

I glanced back at my wife, still deep in conversation with Mrs. Royston, and my two children who had all their tomorrows to look forward to. There were no more stories left for either Royston or myself to exchange. Looked at objectively, the visit had been a success. In spite of all that had happened during the intervening years, everything was serene in the West's home at Walton-on-Thames, just as if the Second World War had never been. I realised there was no future to be had reliving my past. I got up and with a conscious gesture turned my back on the river. Royston followed suit and nodded across to the Anglers Arms.

'How about a pint before you go? The landlord's still the same.'

Nostalgically, I remembered the innkeeper and his jocular reference to Mr. West as Mr. Billy-boy. It was only years later I learned that a Billy-boy was a barge-like coaster and that in view of his stature the publican may have decided it was an apt nickname for his corpulent neighbour across the water. I shook my head.

'I'd like to, Royston, but one pint will lead to another, and I'm driving.'

We said goodbye to his wife and he walked with us to our car. Just as we were about to drive off he suddenly clasped his forehead.

'Good lord! I almost forgot! I've something here of yours.'

He dashed back into the house and returned with a small bundle which he thrust through the open window into my lap.

'They were still on the engine when *Ammonatis* was salvaged.'

I looked at the swimming trunks and remembered Jamie MacDougal promising to keep them safe from moths. Royston stood by the car with a boyish grin on his face.

'After you left I only saw him wear them once. It was when he came back after the war. You'd never have guessed it but he had skinny legs. What with him having shaved off his beard, you wouldn't have recognised him.'

I couldn't account for it but I was depressed as we waved a last farewell and drove away. As we crossed Walton Bridge on the way back to London I knew I would never return. It wasn't only a question of acknowledging the old saw that it was wiser to leave memories undisturbed than try to recreate them. Perhaps more than anything, what made up my mind was the wish to preserve my memories of the one character who for me was the personification of a naval hero; a Drake, Raleigh and Nelson combined in one person. I wanted to remember Jamie MacDougal as I remembered him – not standing at the wheel of *Ammonatis* smooth-faced and spindly-legged in my moth-eaten swimming trunks, but a magnificent figure just like the bearded sailor who fronted the packet of John Player's cigarettes.

A STRIKING RESEMBLANCE

Some of the strangest aspects of my life have been its coincidences. Often they have been bizarre enough to challenge the laws of chance and suggest something more ordained. As a committed atheist-cum-agnostic-humanist I can hardly go so far as to mention fate or faith, but the odds against some events coming about are truly astronomical.

The most dramatic coincidence happened during the last war. It began in 1940 when I was posted from my unit in Sussex to complete a six-week 'instructors' course in Harrogate, Yorkshire. At the time I was an NCO in a rifle regiment, and wore, as part of my uniform, a khaki beret with a green hackle fastened above the eye. For reasons never stated by the military authorities, the hat had to be worn so both ears were free. Perhaps the experts were convinced that this way alert riflemen would hear the bomb, bullet or shell aimed at him and have time to duck.

In the traitorous cause of individualism, I wore the cloth cap covering the right ear. I can't say why I chose to stand out from the unformed crowd this idiosyncratic way, except I know at the time sartorial opportunities were strictly limited. It certainly had nothing to do with bombardment of any kind. I possessed no death wish. On the contrary, I had a strong sense of survival. It possibly occurred to me at the time that one ear was enough.

The day the course assembled, I listened attentively as the Colonel outlined our programme for the coming six weeks. During the few minutes he took to impress on us the importance of the course and its eventual effect in bringing Hitler's defeat, I was conscious of an unbroken stare from a sergeant standing near me. Awareness gave way to irritation as the Colonel was followed by his adjutant who got down to the practical military business of allocating beds, blankets and instructors.

It was while unpacking a little later that the staring sergeant came into my room and without a word of explanation or introduction, took a photograph from his pocket and handed it to me.

There was no mistaking who it was. It was me. How this stranger had a print was beyond my understanding. He watched my face closely. 'It's my young brother,' he said.

I stared at the photograph and felt strangely deflated. Like all young vain people, up to that moment I'd regarded myself as uniquely individual. Now here I was, dressed in the same uniform – the hat 'incorrectly' covering one ear – and it was not me at all.

It transpired that the young man, like me, had been drafted into the same regiment, but posted to the 1st Battalion, whereas I was with the second. As a result of this outlandish coincidence, the sergeant and I became friends for the duration of the course and though we got on well for six weeks, in truth we had little in common except neither of us passed with flying colours and whatever instruction we'd received it made no difference whatsoever to Hitler or his armies.

Before we parted to go back to our separate units we promised to keep in touch, as wartime acquaintances invariably do, but predictably we never even exchanged one letter. Even before I was back in the cradle of my unit I had put the sergeant and my other self out of mind.

Germane to this story is the fact that I had, at this time, an elder brother stationed, as all were in those secretive military days, somewhere in England. In appearance, two brothers couldn't have been more unlike. I was of medium height, slim, clean-shaven, light of skin – a round-faced, immature, underdeveloped adult of 22 years. In contrast my brother stood over 6ft, weighed 17 stone, was dark-skinned and heavily moustached – looking nearer 35 than 27.

Yet one year after the Harrogate incident, in 1941, my brother wrote to say he'd been recognised by the self-same sergeant. It had happened at another assembly depot, this time the meeting ground for volunteers for the newly formed Reconnaissance Corps. As a result of the extraordinary double coincidence the two men struck up a firm friendship.

In spite of the fact that for the following 12 months we were all still stationed in England, we never managed to meet together, not even to say goodbye when my brother's unit was posted overseas to India. In the months that followed, letters arrived with snapshots; always the two friends side by side. By 1942, the postal designation had changed from 'somewhere in the Far East' to 'somewhere in the Near East'; later it became 'somewhere in the Middle East'. By that time I was corresponding from 'somewhere in North Africa'. Militarily our paths were converging. Thus are modern wars conducted. I became increasingly certain we were due for a grand reunion 'somewhere in Central Mediterranean'. There seemed an inevitable, fateful pattern to events that had started in Yorkshire three years before.

We did in fact converge on the same military point but alas without a reunion. In fact, we weren't even aware of one another's presence. The next information concerning my brother came via my wife in England to tell me he had been killed in the battle for Catania and was buried 'somewhere in Sicily'. It was July 1943. I tried to contact his unit to learn the details of his death in action but failed. By that time the Recce Corps were involved in other battles – meaning other casualties.

Late in 1944, in a small town east of Naples, a sergeant major walked into my office, glanced searchingly at my face and wordlessly came across to shake my hand. I glanced at his hat badge and recognised his unit. It was an emotional moment.

It transpired that the Catania campaign was the unit's first battle action.

A sortie of two reconnaissance vehicles went ahead of the main force. They comprised of my brother in one vehicle and the sergeant friend in another. Perched on the hill overlooking the plane, the Sergeant Major and the rest could see what the two vehicle commanders couldn't – German artillery trained on them.

They never knew what hit them. He puffed hard on his cigarette and inhaled deeply. 'We had to wait till dark to get them. There wasn't much left.' For a moment he pretended smoke had got into his eye.

Listening to the details a year and a half after the event, it seemed impersonal and commonplace; the sort of wartime story one had heard countless times before.

When he'd finished his cigarette he rose, shook my hand again and left. I didn't ask his name, there seemed little point. I sat for a time thinking less on the details of my brother's and his friend's death then on the odds against this sergeant major stumbling across me in an Italian outpost. It seemed too coincidental to be true.

Many years later I visited the military cemetery in Catania. There lying beside my brother was a gravestone with Sergeant Todd's name engraved on it. I never knew if his younger brother who looked exactly like me survived the war.

THE IMPRESARIO
FROM LITTLE VENICE

I first met Jim Crocker during the closing months of the Second World War. He was 22 years old and newly conscripted into HM Forces, having been deferred earlier call-up due to university studies in art and philosophy. At least that was the story he told. To someone like me, who'd spent the previous six years in khaki, he seemed very boyish, with reddish hair atop a round, chinless, smooth-skinned face. Just why the authorities felt it necessary to post an arts degree graduate to a theatre of war when the fighting was practically over in Europe remained a minor mystery.

But he was jolly company, with an infectious laugh, and saw the humorous side of life. He made fun of everyone and everything military but it was impossible to be offended by him. During the months he was with us, I often wondered whether lecturers and tutors at London University found his irreverence and flippancy as amusing as we did or whether both traits reduced them to impatience and academic frustration.

There was only one thing that moved him to seriousness and that was art. Then he was a mine of information and completely transformed. To those of us who'd never set foot in an art gallery or museum it wasn't so much his knowledge that held our interest but the performance he gave when talking about it. On these occasions, he was like an orchestral conductor as he expressed his admiration of the great painters and their creations. Using arms, hands and fingers to paint imaginary illustrations, our ignorance of the masters only inspired him to great emotion as he went into enthusiastic detail about them.

'Take Canaletto, for example.' At that he'd hold one arm at full length, close an eye and with his thumb point ahead as if measuring perspectives, the better to emphasise his admiration for the Italian painter and his subject. 'The canals in his paintings of Venice look so real you could imagine you were on the water in a gondola looking at the churches either side of the banks.'

Unmindful of our total ignorance of the Italian artist and his paintings of the watery city, without pause he'd switch to another legendary artist.

'Then there's Turner's paintings in Essex.' Again he'd mime an emotion, this time looking up at the barrack-room ceiling with an expression of wonderment. 'He painted skies so real you could imagine the clouds were actually moving along on the canvas.' He'd then moved his hand rapidly back and forth as if making a series of wide brush strokes. 'It looks simple till you try and paint them yourself. Then you appreciate how difficult it is and what a genius he was at catching the light.'

On the occasion of him admitting his inability to paint like Turner, it prompted an innocent query from one of the members of our company.

'Done some painting yourself then?'

To Jim Crocker the question was an affront of outrageous proportions. His eyes almost popped from their sockets

'Done some painting myself?!' As if to dismiss the questioner with contempt, he did a mime of an artist standing before an easel at work on some imaginary canvas. 'You don't think I was a gold medallist at the Academy of Modern Art for nothing?! They don't hand them out just because you're a pretty face.'

That information said it all for us. In spite of his boyish

humour there was more to him than we'd realised, which to me made his posting to a military unit like ours seem more ludicrous than before. Here was a gifted young man and his expertise was being wasted on useless military routines. The authorities should have considered putting his skills to better use, commissioning him as a war artist maybe, in the hope and expectation he'd develop into a painter of renown and not only be a credit to the British Army but to the United Kingdom.

It was only days after his emotional revelation about himself as a painter of outstanding talent that the private soldier who'd unintentionally provoked the outburst caused an even greater reaction from him. Impressed that the 'chinless wonder' was more worthy of respect than he'd been shown before, during a tea break in the NAAFI canteen the questioning soldier brought along a sketch pad and box of paints and plonked them down on the table in front of him.

'Here you are, Jim boy. We all clubbed together.'

The flush that flooded Crocker's cheeks almost matched the ginger hair of his head and there was a slight tremble to his hands as he opened the lid and surveyed the row of paints set in their white ceramic holders. My initial thought was that he was overcome with emotion at the generous gift and for the first time in our experience was too overcome to speak. The soldier also took it as a sign of appreciation.

'It's so's you can paint us a picture we could put up on the barrack-room wall!'

Then came the unexpected surprise. With a firm decisive action, Jim Crocker closed the lid of the box and handed it back to the soldier.

'It's real nice of you and the others to go to this trouble and expense, and I'd like to accept the gift, but I can't. It wouldn't be fair.'

We all looked puzzled but it was left to the soldier to express our bewilderment.

'What do you mean not fair?'

'These are water colours. If I'd known you were going to buy them I'd have told you before. I only paint in oils.'

He held out the box of paints with a look of genuine regret. There was a stunned silence. None of us knew a different technique was involved in painting pictures, and his specialised information of the subject put him on an even higher plane of admiration than before. But then, as the soldier took the paint box back, with surprising persistence he pointed to the sketch pad.

'Draw something instead. One of the RSM! We'll put it up on the wall and use it as a dartboard.'

From the slow shake of Jim Crocker's head it was clear he was on firm ground with an expertise that couldn't be challenged or denied.

'I'd like to be a Leonardo Da Vinci or a Rembrandt but water and clouds – that's what I do best, that's what I won a prize for. I couldn't draw a face to save my life. You could draw one better than I could.'

The frankness and honesty with which he admitted his technical limitations was impossible to challenge. He'd made it clear his artistic idols were those who excelled at painting water and sky, therefore it was logical for him to model himself on them. That was the last time during the rest of our military service together that anyone asked him to put his artistic skills to the test.

When the war was finally won and the defeated German hierarchy signed the surrender document on Lüneburg

Heath, we all went back to being civilians again. Apart from friendships sworn to be kept going and promises to meet annually at regimental reunions, in truth there was small chance of our paths ever crossing again. The likelihood of meeting Jim Crocker in particular was even more remote. Even if he did become recognised as an outstanding talent he'd be moving in circles far different from mine, and except for pure social snobbery there'd be no justification to contact him as a painting celebrity in the tradition of Turner and Canaletto. But fate moves in mysterious ways and never more so than in this particular case.

It was almost five years after being demobilised that the wildly unexpected reunion with Jim Crocker took place. In 1950, the euphoria of being a civilian was long gone. Memories of the war with its fears and excitements, frustrations and boredom, were replaced by feelings of responsibility and worry of supporting a wife and family. Military life had much against it but it provided board, lodging, clothes and paid leaves. In peacetime one had to work and earn a living to pay for the equivalents and the term duration meant for the rest of one's life not just till the end of hostilities. One way or another it tended to have a depressing effect.

Since being demobilised in 1946, I'd reached the rank of factory foreman in the cabinet industry and my peacetime uniform consisted of a brown cloth coat. Mercifully, the traditional bowler that went with it as an insignia of status and authority had been discarded and it was left to me as a former senior NCO to exercise control over the stroppy union-dominated shop floor operatives. More than 20 years were to pass before decimalisation took place and many after that when inflation took off like a rocket, but in 1950, after five years hard effort, my salary had reached £7 and 10 shillings per week. Relative to today's prices, a foreman would average £250–300 per week depending on the fortunes or otherwise of the industry he was in.

It was against my inauspicious career with its rut-like future that the unexpected reunion with Jim Crocker took place. It came out of the blue with a telephone call from him one Saturday afternoon in 1950. The sound of his happy-go-lucky voice conjured an instant image of the ebullient youthful soldier, and within seconds the memory of the cheery humorous young man came flooding back. His opening greeting was true to character.

'Is that you, Staff?'

There was no preamble explaining how he'd traced me to my flat in Islington.

'Private Jim Crocker?'

'As was. As was.'

'Well, bless my soul!'

It was all I could think to say but it didn't matter. A compulsive talker by nature, he made the running.

'I don't know about you, Staff, but I'm dead keen to meet up again. It's been a long time. I've lots to tell you.'

My mind raced with what that might be. I'd taken to scanning reviews for mention of up-and-coming artists just in case I'd see his name.

'Are you a famous painter yet?'

'Not so's you'd notice. But I'll tell you all about it when we meet up, whenever that can be – and where.'

My wife was standing nearby, curious to know who I was speaking to. I cupped the mouthpiece and swiftly explained it was an old army friend and could I invite him over. She nodded.

'Come to lunch tomorrow.'

'Tomorrow? That's great!'

'It's 54 Brunswick Terrace, behind King's Cross mainline railway station. One o'clock sharp.'

'One o'clock it is, Staff! I'll be there spick and span.'

The way he rattled off the instruction was like a squaddie repeating a military detail. I knew my wife would be bored by wartime reminiscences and I didn't relish being constantly referred to by my ex-army rank.

'By the way, Jim, I'm a civilian now, not a senior NCO. There's no need to be formal. My first name's Henry.'

'OK, Staff. Hal it is!'

The unexpected familiarity took me by surprise.

'Tomorrow – one o'clock on the dot. See you then.'

And with that he hung up. My wife was still standing near, waiting to be filled in with details about tomorrow's surprise guest.

'Private Jim Crocker. A soldier in my old outfit. He was known to everyone as the chinless wonder on account of his round, smooth baby-face without a hair on it.' She was patient as I gave a fuller description. 'He was a military misfit. We tried to make him look and act like a soldier but it was a complete waste of time. Really, he was just a 22-year-old overgrown schoolboy. But a talented overgrown schoolboy for all that.'

'Talented?'

'He paints pictures. He's an artist. You'll like him.'

My wife was unimpressed by showy people with affected airs and I was confident when she saw Jim Crocker's ordinariness and listened to his good-humoured chaff she'd be won over by him as we all were in the army unit in 1945. If anything I expected her to feel motherly towards him even though they were both about the same age. In the summer of 1950 I didn't think that I'd made a mistake inviting him to our flat for Sunday lunch.

The area bordering King's Cross railway termini today is not what it was in 1950 when the ravages of Hitler's blitzkrieg were still in evidence, and Brunswick Terrace not a terrace in the true sense of the word because there were gaps in it where houses used to be. Looking down the street in one direction we could see the rear of the mainline grimy sheds and in another the cast-iron holders of the local gasworks. When the wind favoured north or south the smells coming from both directions were less than pleasant. But my wife and I were fortunate to have accommodation and not live with either set of parents and the rent of 30 shillings a week was within our budget.

That Sunday, 50 years ago, was still a day of comparative quiet, at least as far as traffic was concerned. Owning and running a motorcar was beyond the means of the working class and the day of door-to-door travel had yet to dawn. In 1950, people took the tube, bus or tram to a convenient fare stage and then walked on to their final destination. Looking out along Brunswick Terrace we could see a quarter of a mile to the road fronting the railway station and when they were within reasonable distance identify whoever it was coming to visit us.

At ten minutes to one, I took up a position at the window and waited to catch sight of the chinless wonder as he made his way towards number 54. I could see people coming away from the terminus and making off in different directions but only a handful walking down Brunswick Terrace. Even from a quarter of a mile away one figure stood out from the rest. It would have stood out in Piccadilly Circus or Trafalgar Square. Though the Sun was shining and the weather warm, the man had a light fawn cape slung over his shoulders and a wide-brimmed sombrero-style velour hat set at a 30-degree angle to his face. To complete the ensemble he held a malacca cane in his right hand which he manoeuvred rhythmically as he strode along with an athletic and purposeful stance. Most astonishingly of all, his face was almost entirely obscured by a reddish-brown beard.

The apparition was so outlandish for the slummy street behind King's Cross station that I called to my wife who was putting cutlery on the dining-room table.

'Quick, Jeannie. Come and see this!'

The urgency in my voice had her concerned.

'What is it? Not an accident?'

'Not an accident. An apparition.' I pointed to the strange figure striding along. 'How about that for King's Cross? Or anywhere else I shouldn't wonder!'

With no more neighbourly contact that an elderly widow on one side of 54 and a derelict house the other, I had to assume the outlandish character was making for gasometer territory behind the terrace; a fact which made the bizarre figure even more ludicrously out of place. My wife, who was more concerned setting her table than commenting on the sight that so intrigued me, turned from the window and left for the kitchen. She wasn't there when the figure stopped and to my astonishment rang the front doorbell.

Five years is an age in many respects but generally speaking young adults don't change very dramatically, not unless they're Dr. Jekyll or Mr. Hyde. Certainly not people like the chinless wonder. But that's who the apparition was. When I opened the door the cheery voice emanating from the mass of ginger facial hair confirmed without doubt that it was the former Private Jim

Crocker. He slipped the cane under his armpit like an officer preparing to return a salute and held out his free hand.

'Hello, Staff – I mean, Hal. Great to see you!'

I shook his hand but I was in a daze. He stood back for me to admire his outfit, unaware I'd been following his progress from King's Cross road to my doorstep.

'What do you think? Better than battledress?'

It was just as well I'd called my wife to the window when I did. The shock of seeing him for the first time when I introduced them would have been too much for her. As it was, she kept her cool and served lunch as if he was one of our usual Sunday lunchtime guests. Fortunately, whatever else had changed about Jim Crocker's appearance, the man himself hadn't. His penchant for holding forth about a subject close to his heart was unaffected and undiminished. In this case the subject was himself. At one stage during the meal he stroked his luxuriant beard.

'Do you know why I grew this?' I knew from previous experience he never waited for answers to his own rhetorical questions. 'Chaps in the platoon were right to call me a baby-face chinless wonder because that's exactly what I was. But there's only one drawback with a distinguished fuzz like mine – it doesn't go with flannel bags and a blazer. People with flowing beards have always had this problem. Augustus John, Count Tolstoy, Bernard Shaw – they all had to deal with it. And they did so by dressing the part. I decided if it was all right for them it was all right for me. The man you see is still Jim Crocker, only now he looks like what he is – an artist, a painter of pictures.'

It was a bravura performance. I was impressed by it but I could tell my wife was put out that he should have bracketed himself with famous people even though she'd never read a word of Tolstoy or Shaw and couldn't identify a work by any well-known painter. Moreover, the bearded wonder didn't make her feel motherly towards him as I'd predicted. In fact, I was relieved when she cleared the table, leaving us alone together. Even then the flamboyant ex-private was a man of surprises. He took a leather case from inside his velvet corduroy jacket and a long-stemmed holder from its pocket. All his movements were deliberately exaggerated. Then with a flourish he inserted a slim panatela cigar, lit up and sat puffing contentedly as he smiled at me. With memories and mental images of the callow soldier who was such a hopeless misfit in an infantry platoon, the character sitting facing me seemed even more miscast.

There was no need for me to prompt him with questions about the five years since we were last together. He said he wanted to meet and swap stories, but the truth was he wanted to talk about himself, which was a relief to me. In one respect our roles were reversed. While I was involved in a routine and monotonous job, he appeared to have attained heights of creative activity. Secretly I felt envious of his lifestyle and even though there was nothing I could have said or done that afternoon that would have stopped him, I was willing to act the host and leave Jim Crocker to hold the floor.

'I tell you, Hal, life wasn't easy being a civilian. I soon used up my army gratuity buying paints and scavenging bits of cardboard for canvases. Even great artists need to keep their hand in and practice their craft, and two years without painting anything made it hard for me to earn a crust.'

The down-to-earth expression seemed strangely at odds with his appearance. As I studied his expensive clothes I concluded earning a crust meant much more to him than it did to me. I remained silent and let him continue.

'I followed the traditional path of a struggling artist in an attic. It was above a fish shop in Lisson Grove. During the terrible winter of 1947, I nearly froze to death. I'd have starved too if it hadn't been for the owner helping out with cod and chips in exchange for one or two sketches. And then in 1948 my fortunes changed very much for the better.'

'You sold some canvases and made a crust?'

'I met a patron of the arts.'

The news surprised me. The only facts I knew about artists subsidised by benefactors came from him when he told of the Vatican paying Michelangelo to paint the Sistine Chapel and Venetian Doges doing the same for artists during the Italian Renaissance. But I couldn't imagine the Archbishop of Canterbury or the Cardinal of Westminster fulfilling a similar role for an unknown painter who on conscription registered as an atheist rather than CE or RC. Before I could ask about his guardian angel he cut across my thoughts.

'I was able to move from the smell of frying oil and work where the air was clean, to Little Venice in Maida Vale. It was where Adrian had his houseboat.'

It was irrational on my part but my eyebrows raised though I tried not to look shocked. In the months we'd been billeted together I'd never suspected his sexual orientation; now it occurred to me that the respect he'd shown during his service wasn't of a private for his senior NCO but of a man attracted physically. Suddenly, I felt uncomfortable and regretted the lunchtime reunion. For his part, Jim Crocker was perfectly at ease.

'It isn't that Adrian isn't talented in his own right. He does wonders with interior designs and decorations but I'm a surrogate to his desires to paint murals and portraits. That's why he's supporting me. In a way we're soulmates rather than patron and struggling artist.'

At that moment of intimacy I was relieved my wife Jeannie was in the kitchen washing plates. Whether he'd have been as forthcoming if she'd been with us I couldn't judge, but one thing was certain; had he mentioned the relationship with his benefactor she'd have left the room. It was 15 years before Wolfenden put an end to the social taboos and legal constraints on homosexuality – long before they started boasting about their sexual differences.

'You'd appreciate Adrian, Hal. He's a military type. I'd like you two to meet one day. You'd have lots in common.'

The conversation was becoming too personal for comfort and I wanted to end it. Whether my wife was psychic and sensed this or had her fill of his conversation over lunch, after a few minutes she rejoined us and pointed to the mantlepiece clock.

'You won't forget, Henry, we promised my parents we'd join them for tea. I'm sure your friend James will understand why we have to cut his visit short.' She turned to Jim Crocker with a smile but it was forced. 'They live in St. Albans. We have to catch a train.'

In a flash he was on his feet, a model of sensitivity, anxious not to outstay his welcome. He didn't show a flicker of emotion at her referring to him as my friend or calling him by his formal name instead of Jim. Instead, and to her great surprise, he grasped her hand and held it to him in a gesture of affection and appreciation.

'My dear Jean, I understand completely. It was good of you and Hal to put up with me for so long. I hope I'll soon have the pleasure of returning your hospitality.'

After our goodbyes and promises to meet up again, my wife and I stood by the window and watched him swagger down Brunswick Terrace towards King's Cross. The truth was we weren't due to go to St. Albans. My wife's parents lived a few streets from us, behind the gasometers where her father worked during the week. I made no mention of his homosexual benefactor or hinted at his barely concealed attraction for me. I just felt a sense of relief at being spared his intimate conversation. But for all that I was still intrigued by the larger-than-life character he'd become. His story of exchanging paintings for cod and chips was life copying art. Puccini's poet in *La bohème* did much the same to keep warm in a cold attic. It was even possible that the bearded Jim Crocker might blossom into a great and famous artist so that art-ignorant people like myself and wife Jeannie would get to know and appreciate his genius.

It is too long ago now to pinpoint the exact month or day that I got the second telephone call from him. I know it was more than a year after the King's Cross reunion, perhaps longer – 1951 or 52. For whatever reason that prevented it – and secretly I was greatly relieved – we never received a return invitation to lunch as he'd promised. During that period, whenever Jeannie referred to the fact, it was with a sour expression and disapproving voice.

'Whatever you saw in him in the army I can't for the life of me fathom. Who wears a cape and uses a walking stick in King's Cross? And that beard for God's sake! You only had to take one look to see he was phoney.'

I felt hurt and diminished by her criticism. It reflected on my judgement and feeling for the man.

'The man's an artist. Painters don't look like bank clerks.'

'How do you know he's an artist? Because he says so? You've never seen anything he's painted.'

It was true I'd taken on trust all he claimed to be. Not even when the platoon bought him paints did it result in a single brushstroke from him. And I couldn't prove his story of exchanging landscapes for fried fish in Lisson Grove. At one stage of her outburst I considered mentioning Adrian in Little Venice as proof of his gifts but thought better of it. As things worked out, it was just as well.

His telephone call came very late one night. The piercing bell woke us both and disturbed our young baby sleeping in a cot in our room. As my wife soothed her she looked anxious, fearful that it concerned her ageing parents. I could think of no one who'd telephone me in the small hours. When I lifted the receiver by my bedside table and heard the raucous voice, I swiftly cupped the mouthpiece. It was a reflex action on my part. It wasn't to shield him from the noise of the whimpering child but to prepare Jeannie for the shock. Even at the best of times, a mention of the flamboyant character produced an intolerant response. In her present emotional state I knew very well what her reaction would be. I whispered his name.

'It's Jim Crocker!'

Instead of relief that it wasn't a family crisis, she stared back at me with a look combining incredulity and outrage.

'For God's sake!

Even as she put the baby back in the cot she spoke so loudly I was sure he must have heard.

'Tell him he's no right to disturb people this time of night. You're not a layabout like him. You have to work for a living. We all have responsibilities.'

I turned away from her as far as the phone would reach. It seemed unreasonable for me to berate him after all these years, even if it was an unreasonable time.

'What is it, Jim?'

The torrent of words that flowed from him gave me the impression he was either drunk or there was extreme atmospheric interference on the line. It was only after seconds piecing together the garbled and disjointed conversation that I realised he was in a highly disturbed and emotional state and probably under the influence of alcohol or drugs. As it transpired, the dramatic call was very short. Without waiting for any comment from me, quite suddenly he rang off. When I replaced the receiver the only sound in the room was my wife lulling our daughter's cries to a tired whisper. She looked at me grim-faced.

'What on earth did he want ringing this time of night?'

I looked at her for several seconds, quite speechless. I was trying to come to terms with the aborted conversation.

'He said he'd just slashed all his paintings because none were any good and there was nothing left but to end it all. He rang to say goodbye before he drowned himself!'

I expected Jeannie to feel remorse at the depressing news but there wasn't a flicker of reaction from her. Instead she was very calm and surprisingly practical.

'Dial 999. The police will go to his place and stop him.'

It was that advice that brought home the full import of the tragic situation. I didn't know which houseboat in Little Venice belonged to Jim Crocker's patron Adrian, nor even his telephone number. Phoning 999 and calling the police or ambulance was as hopeless as making for Maida Vale and searching the canal for a red-bearded corpse. Sleep for the rest of the night was out of the question. I was haunted by visions of him floating on the Grand Union Canal and feelings of sadness combined with guilt engulfed me. The particular thought that kept recurring was of the irony that a man obsessed with depicting water like his idol Canaletto should end his young life drowning in it.

By daybreak I was in two minds whether to report for work as usual or go to Little Venice asking at each moored houseboat about a midnight suicide. In the end I decided against Maida Vale. I was put off by the possibility of coming face to face with Jim Crocker's patron and embarrassed at the ex-captain bewailing his lover's death. It was cowardly of me not to do the decent thing and it bothered me for days afterwards. Instead I searched the local papers for news of a drowning but found no mention of any.

It's said that time's a great healer, and as far as Jim Crocker's suicide was concerned, in a year or so all thoughts of the late failed artist of Maida Vale had gone from my mind. By the summer of 1953 my situation had improved considerably and Jeannie and I moved from King's Cross to a suburb in Essex. It was there one weekend when I answered my front door and saw him standing smiling at me that I was not only shocked by the fact of his survival but also by his changed appearance. Gone was the sombrero set at a rakish angle, the billowing cape draped over a corduroy jacket and a malacca cane held like an RSM Coldstream Guard's measuring stick. Facing me with a wide boyish smile on his hairless face was the original chinless wonder of wartime memory. It was as if I was in a time warp. He was dressed in grey flannel trousers and a blue blazer with a regimental badge on the breast pocket. In a slight daze I invited him in and called out to my wife to come and see who the caller was. This time he received a more welcoming reception. Jeannie was equally surprised to see him but gone from her face was any sign of hostility. Possibly the sight of his cheerful baby-face stirred latent maternal instincts in her as I suggested they might on his first visit seven years before.

Without any explanation for his uninvited arrival or changed appearance he started jabbering away about the exciting events that had happened to him since we last met several years ago. He made no reference to his work as an artist or anything about the patron of Little Venice. Nor was there was any mention of his late-night suicidal phone call and I took it as confirmation that he was so high on some drug or other when he made the threat that he had no conscious memory of it. For both omissions I was greatly relieved. The one piece of information he held to the last was the most surprising. It was when he said he was a theatrical impresario putting on plays in the West End of London that for several seconds I stared at him speechless.

Not only was I bewildered by the news, I was intrigued to know what had happened to the modern-day Turner; the potential genius obsessed with reproducing land and seascapes that would rival his other idol, Canaletto. Searching my mind for a possible explanation to this incredible change in lifestyle, it occurred to me he might be deliberately avoiding any mention of destroying his canvases and threatening suicide; that even after all these years he was still traumatised by the event and his present superficial chat was a psychological cover-up for his embittered frustration and wounded psyche. As if reading my mind, he quickly dispelled such Freudian thoughts with an honest and logical explanation of the reasons for the change. It was made without embarrassment or emotion.

'You know, sometimes it's a trivial incident that changes your life forever. Maybe a casual remark made by a stranger or something one reads in a book. That's how it was with me. When I learned it was Bernard Shaw who said people should do what they could with their lives not what they dreamed of doing the message really struck a chord. I took a hard look at myself and even harder look at my work and came to the conclusion that, Academy gold medallist or not, if I practised for the rest of my life I'd never be a Canaletto or a Turner. My paintings didn't look as if they'd been done by a master artist or even a talented one. It came home to me with blinding clarity that what the great GBS said in general applied to me in particular. Whether I liked it or not, it was a fact of life that what I was really good at was talking about art, not reproducing it. In other words, put crudely, I had the gift of the gab and what I should do was to use that natural talent to achieve my ambitions. Since that conversion that's precisely what I have been doing, and very successfully too I'm happy to say.'

It was very strange hearing him talk so objectively and self-critically about himself. When I knew him in the army he was not given to introspection. I recalled his lectures about art and artists and the effect his enthusiasm had even on the semi-literate members of our platoon. There was no doubting the fact that, as he said with such frankness, he had the gift of the gab, and apparently better able to profit from it than daubing away trying to reproduce images of sea and sky on cardboard canvases. It was also apparent he was a changed person from the tormented character who last spoke to me of doing away with himself. While mulling on the strangeness of his unpredictable and unconventional life, for the second time that morning he broke into my thoughts.

'The people where you used to live in King's Cross gave me your address. I thought I'd surprise you. It was worth coming all the way out to Ongar just to see you and Jean. I knew you'd be pleased I came.'

'Very pleased, Jim.'

At that moment I truthfully meant it.

'Not that talking about myself was the main reason I came.'

If anything, the sudden note of mystery made me suspicious.

'Not the main reason?'

'I'm not the selfish type who forgets old friends.'

Almost as if she shared my feelings of doubt at his cryptic remarks, Jeannie decided it was time to leave us alone together and go off to make tea. It was only when she was out of the room that Jim Crocker made clear the true purpose of his visit to our semi in suburban Essex. He leaned forward in his chair and assumed an exaggerated air of conspiratorial confidentiality.

'You know what is meant by being an angel, Henry?'

It was the first time he used my first name and I sensed there was purpose to it. He didn't wait for me to answer.

'It's the title given to investors who put up money to produce plays in the theatre and films in the cinema.'

In spite of our worlds being poles apart, I was nonetheless familiar with the term. I nodded.

'Well, you're going to have the chance to be one!'

He chose to ignore my look of utter incomprehension. Instead he gave a swift glance around the empty room as if someone might have slipped in unnoticed, then in the same hushed voice continued.

'Before I say another word about it, Hal, you've got to promise me something.'

He didn't wait for a reply or even a nod of agreement.

'What I have to tell you must be kept to yourself – and your wife Jeannie, naturally – it's that hush-hush. At the moment only a handful of people know about it.'

He stared hard at me, looking deadly serious.

'You promise?'

'I promise.'

He leaned back in his chair and relaxed as though relieved of a huge burden.

'No names, no pack-drill, Hal, but a very well-known playwright is putting on a new production in the West End of London and willing to let a few people fund the enterprise – in other words, be angels. That's the reason I've come to see you today. I thought you more than anyone I know deserved to have the chance to share in this golden opportunity.'

He folded his arms across his chest and sat smiling at me with shining eyes. It was his smug self-satisfied manner as much as the mind-bending offer that convinced me he'd been speaking the truth when he said his life had changed as a result of George Bernard Shaw's advice; that after wasted years as a struggling artist he'd replaced that misplaced dedication with a career as an impresario and was a success at it because that's where his natural talents lay.

It was in this new-found role in his life that he was now in my Ongar home to convince me to invest money in an artistic venture regardless of being aware of how far removed I was from his esoteric milieu and how little I knew about theatre or film production. But for all the fact that there was absolutely no possibility of my participating in what he glowingly referred to as a golden opportunity, nonetheless I felt a grudging admiration for his salesman's technique in appealing both to my vanity and sense of greed and at the same time playing on my natural curiosity. I was keen to know more of the identity of the famous playwright and the details of the specialised financing. In spite of him including Jeannie as confidante in the secret plan, I was anxious to hear all about it before she rejoined us with tea.

'It's true, Jim, I've improved myself quite a bit since King's Cross, but for all that I'm not well heeled, not as you may think I am. No way am I rich enough to be an angel.'

He leaned forward in his chair and gripped my knee with one hand. I recognised the gesture was evidence of his earnestness in the theatrical enterprise but my thoughts went back to the houseboat in Little Venice and his patron Adrian, and involuntarily I withdrew my legs from his reach. I was uneasy at his touch but he took no exception and continued to appeal more intensely than before.

'This is a once-in-a-lifetime proposition, Henry. It's the times we're in that's making it so. Probably there'll never be another such offer. We're not talking big money, just a modest outlay to acquire a share in a fabulous opportunity.'

I was intrigued by the suggestion that it was within my means.

'A modest outlay?'

'Nothing on a grand scale.'

He could tell my appetite was whetted.

'A mere £100.'

Writing this account of events virtually at the beginning of the third millennium that sum seems ludicrous, but in 1953 my salary was £20 a week before deductions. A 'mere' £100 represented more than a month's pay. The equivalent figure today would be in the region of £2,500. I had neither capital saved nor wealthy friends to borrow money from. I shook my head.

'I'm sorry, Jim, it's beyond my means. Way beyond.'

He brushed my comment aside as if he'd anticipated it and instead came up with an instant solution.

'Take a mortgage on your house!'

'I already have one on it.'

His voice grew more urgent.

'Take another! If necessary borrow the money. How about friends or relations? They'll get a bigger return on capital than they could get from a building society or cooperative bank – much bigger.'

He changed tactics and instead of appealing to me as one old friend to another adopted a more accusatory manner.

'If those close to you ever got to know you denied them the opportunity to benefit from this proposition they could take the view that you did so deliberately and take exception to it. Take you and me for instance. If I'd denied you the chance to make a bundle and you found out about it you'd feel I'd let you down after all we'd been to one another. In your case it could poison relationships with in-laws. It might even cause friction between you and Jean.'

Even as I half wondered if Jeannie's father – a gasworks engineer – could possibly have saved such a nest egg when I knew for certain my bank clerk father hadn't, I couldn't help admiring Jim Crocker for the variations in his money-raising routine. He ignored me and looked around the living room, nodding with appreciation at the furnishings.

'Sell a few possessions. You'll be able to replace reproductions with genuine antiques. You'll recoup your money plus interest in no time at all. I tell you, Hal, it's the chance of a lifetime!'

His enthusiasm and belief in the proposition that an outlay of £100 would yield more than could be expected from any other speculative investment and in a relatively short time was such that had I not been anxious to end the conversation before Jeannie came back, I might have been won over by his passionate plea for the project. I might even have seriously considered raising the money by secretly taking out a second mortgage and keeping the fact from her.

It was the rattle of the tea trolley as she neared the living room that brought me back to earth and convinced me it was time to end the topic of my being a theatrical angel.

'It's no good going on about it, Jim. I can't raise £100 and that's the end of it. I'm not sure I'd want to be an angel even if I had the money to spare. We move in different circles, live different lives. Let's drop the subject before Jeannie comes back with tea. Talking about it will only put her on edge and you wouldn't want to do that.'

'Absolutely not, Hal, old chap. Absolutely not.'

That meeting in 1953 was the first and last time impresario Jim Crocker and I discussed my being an angel either for the well-known playwright's shareholding offer or any other theatrical venture he was involved with. In fact, I never saw or heard from him again after his departure from Ongar. There was an occasion when walking along Piccadilly viewing local artists' exhibits hung on Green Park's railings that I saw an oil painting of a houseboat on Little Venice. There was an old man sitting on a stool nearby who could have been guarding the hundreds of works on show or simply resting from fatigue. I didn't have the pluck to go up and ask him if he was Jim Crocker and the painting his. Anyway, it wasn't very good. But on the odd occasion he does come to mind it's as a round-faced youth with a wide boyish grin – the platoon's chinless wonder of the closing days of the Second World War.

Still, whether he's around or not, the hush-hush project he urged me to join by any means at my disposal is still alive. The angels who pooled their £100s in 1954 enabled the play to be put on in one of London's smallest theatres, and it has been running ever since and has become a theatrical institution. By the most conservative estimate the original investment, if left where it was, would today be worth a thousand times more. As Jim Crocker the born-again impresario prophetically stated, it was the opportunity of a lifetime. Indeed, £100,000 today would be a very nice nest egg for a very old bird.

Who knows what the final dividend might be? Come the millennium and new generations of West End theatre-goers, Agatha Christie's *The Mousetrap* could run another 50 years and become the first ever everlasting play.

AN IDEAL FOREMAN

We were a motley collection. You could meet us anywhere – at a bus stop, in a supermarket or just walking along the street. It was the venue that was unusual, all 20 of us gathered in a courtroom a stone's throw from London's Mansion House and the Bank of England. Viewed from outside it was obvious the City of London Crown Court dated from the time Great Britain ruled the waves and half the world as well. Inside the atmosphere was even more redolent of the empire's glory days. On the morning of the trial, the black-gowned usher who directed us to the jurors room looked very authoritative. When the last of us arrived and numbered 20, she explained why there were more of us called than required for a 12-person jury.

'Counsel mightn't like the look of some of you. They don't say why. It happens when you come to be sworn in.'

She gave no hint who she considered would be rejected.

'That's it then. We can hop it?!'

The black youth with dreadlocks looked 18. He took it for granted that he'd be rejected because of his colour.

'No, sonny Jim, you can't just hop it. At least not till the judge says so.'

I glanced around. If appearances were what counted in the jury selection process it looked as if, along with the black cockney, a young man in trainers and T-shirt, a Sikh in a blue turban and a girl with a ring through her nose might keep him company. Of the others only a distinguished-looking man in a pinstriped suit and old school tie stood out from the rest.

The usher paused at the door.

'Those of you selected will be around for some time. The

chances are this one's going to be a long runner.' Nobody made a comment. 'Of course, if you're taken ill or break a leg you're excused, but not for a cold in the head or a pain in the back. The judge cuts up rough if he thinks jurors are trying it on. Any malingering could be considered as contempt of court.'

It was when she left that the Sikh in the indigo-blue turban looked around and addressed the gathering at large.

'What does that mean – contempt of court?'

The man in the suit seemed well used to answering questions.

'It means you could be punished for not doing your duty.'

'Punished?'

'Reprimanded. Fined. Even put in the cells overnight.'

It was the combination of his formal dress and superior air that immediately impressed the group. Only the youth with the braided hair seemed unconcerned at the penalties a judge could impose on a wayward juror.

'I wouldn't be here in the first place if he knew I was black. You'll see. I'll be the first to be kicked out.'

Several people started to exchange details and complain about what a strain a long trial would have on their domestic and business affairs. One woman wearing wing-shaped spectacles which accentuated her naturally sharp features spoke out more loudly than the rest.

'They've no right to force you to stay if it's going to cause domestic and financial hardship.' There was a general murmur of approval. 'If it comes to it, I'll complain to my MP. We have responsibilities and rights too.'

By her tone of voice and forceful attitude it was hard to imagine her accepting anything that went against her wishes, with or without the assistance of a Member of Parliament.

At her outburst the neatly dressed man made a further objective comment. As before, his voice was calm.

'Madam, instead of complaining, you should consider it a privilege as well as a duty to serve on a jury. You're dealing with a fundamental law of democracy. Trials by one's peers hark back to the middle ages. King John and Magna Carta in the 13th century was the start of it.'

His quiet rebuke combined with a detailed knowledge of English history silenced everyone except the chirpy black youth.

'They never said nothing about Magna Carta in Citizens Advice in Brixton. I went there and told 'em me mum come from Jamaica and I've never seen my old man so what's with this letter telling me to come here?'

The statement was made to the group at large but everyone expected the man in the suit to reply.

'It doesn't matter where your parents came from. You're a British-born adult. That's reason enough to serve as a juror.'

He spoke as a patriot, but of all the group who might have echoed his sentiments it was only the turbaned Sikh who reinforced his point of view.

'Certainly, the gentleman is absolutely right to be proud. This is the most civilised country and Englishmen are most tolerant people. Even those who call me Paki.' He smiled and pointed to his perfectly wound headgear. 'Me, a Paki!'

'We've got Pakis in Hackney. They all stink of curry.'

It was the man in the grubby trainers and soiled T-shirt. His sneering voice was intentionally provocative.

The Sikh stood up in a rage.

'Where I come from all people are clean. No Sikh would come here to court dirty like you.'

The Cockney went red-faced with temper.

'If you don't like it here go back where you came from.'

'I come from Southall!'

The black youth was unconcerned by the angry exchange.

'We've got Paki caffs in Brixton. I like curry.'

I glanced at the man who'd unintentionally created the tense situation, certain he would calm the atmosphere.

'There's no call for anyone to get personal. As the usher said a few moments ago, we might be together for weeks. We need to be tolerant and agreeable towards one another if we're to keep a sense of proportion and exercise fair play in the forthcoming trial.'

There was a nodding of heads and the general consensus was that with his controlled manner and wise words the man in the suit had successfully defused an explosive situation. The English-born Sikh was the first to respond to his appeal.

'You're absolutely correct in what you say, sir. We are in an English court of law and should behave accordingly.'

He looked for a conciliatory response from the man in the T-shirt but he just sat with a vacuous grin on his face and said nothing. Unexpectedly, it was the woman with the glasses who attacked her slovenly compatriot. She turned to him with a fierce expression.

'The man in the turban's right! It's not in keeping to come to a court dressed like you're going to your local.'

She gave a withering look to the young girl by his side.

'Nor is a ring in the nose! The only time I've seen that is on a bull led by a piece of rope. Youngsters today go out of their way to make the worst of themselves.'

The girl gave a sly look with the man in the T-shirt and sniggered with embarrassment. There was no doubt the woman with glasses was as dominant a character as the quietly authoritative man in the suit, but before her abuses to the two people could create a further situation the usher returned.

'OK. We can all go in now. The court's in session. Leave your things here. They'll be safe enough.'

She led the way to the courtroom and directed us to a tier of seats set at right angles to the judge's bench. Almost deferentially the group held back, allowing the man in the suit and the woman with glasses to take their seats in the front row. The Sikh waited till he was sure of sitting furthest from the man in the T-shirt while the girl with a ring in her nose bonded more firmly by sitting next to him. The black youth perched himself right on the end of a row as if ready to exit from the court at the first opportunity. The usher stood to the side of the enclosure, waiting on the court clerk to begin the process of empanelment.

It was my first time in a courtroom and it all seemed very casual. The judge didn't look up from his notes as we took our seats; neither did his clerk riffling through a card index. In the body of the court, several counsels chatted away, turning occasionally to speak to solicitors seated behind them. It was as if we jurors held no interest for any of them. Facing us across the width of the courtroom like an empty pulpit was the witness box and at the rear of the court the prisoner's dock. It was several minutes before the court clerk gathered a sheaf of cards in his hands and nodded to the usher. She turned to face us.

'When the clerk calls out your name, stand up.'

As each name was called the person rose to acknowledge his or her identity and sat down again. I was the fifth to be called. The person most downcast at being selected was the black youth who contrary to expectations wasn't able to 'hop it' back to Brixton. On the other hand, the woman with a ring in her nose and the man in the T-shirt seemed indifferent at being surplus to requirements along with the other six unnamed people.

Once the clerk finished the roll call and put his cards away in the box, the usher took over again.

'Those of you not called aren't excused yet. Just go back to the jury room and wait there.'

As the eight departed there was a general focusing of interest in us by counsel. It was as if by the process of elimination we were now more worthy of attention. It was the female usher standing in front of us who in a quiet voice kept us informed of proceedings.

'When they bring the defendant up from the cells, the clerk will swear you in. I'll give you a card to read from. Just speak up so's the judge can hear you.'

From where we sat there was no indication where the cells were. Suddenly, a man flanked by two policemen appeared and the three men sat down in the dock. From the moment of his arrival the defendant scrutinised each juror in turn. It was as if roles were reversed and we were on trial. When his eyes met mine his piercing gaze was too distracting to outface him and I looked away. Then the clerk of the court took over again.

'When your name is called, the usher will hand you a card. Read from it so that everyone can hear you. If anyone has an objection to taking the oath from the English bible they can affirm or use a bible of their own religion.'

The wording on the card promising to tell the truth and nothing but the truth was so hackneyed most could recite it by heart, yet the necessity to read aloud from the piece of board made some jurors so self-conscious they mumbled and stumbled over the words.

The routine was marginally delayed by the Sikh who affirmed and one juror with a reading problem having to repeat the oath parrot-fashion after the clerk. When the card passed to the black youth he rattled off the words faster than any before him. Seconds later it was my turn but before I could utter a single word I was told by the clerk to stand down. The embarrassment of threading my way past the others and leaving the jury enclosure to return to the waiting room was matched by a feeling of deep humiliation at my unexpected rejection.

Of the eight people sitting there when I returned, only the girl with a ring in her nose chatting away to the man in the T-shirt showed any interest in my reappearance.

'Kicked you out then did they?'

Her cockney voice was devoid of emotion. I nodded, unsure whether to affect indifference or reply and express my feelings, when to my utter amazement the man in the suit and the woman with glasses entered, followed by the usher close behind holding several cards in her hand. Without a moment's delay she called out three names, one of whom was the girl with the nose ring, the second the man in the T-shirt and the third a middle-aged woman. The replacements took place so swiftly that the remaining jurors looked bewildered at the comings and goings, and though not a word was said I had the feeling that by our reappearances we rejected jurors were viewed as somewhat reduced in status. For their part, the other two displayed neither feelings of pique nor inferiority. If anything the man was just as relaxed, though the woman was more indignant than before.

'It's all very well putting you to the inconvenience of coming here in the first place, but then to be rejected like this by the judge! I think it's all a waste of time and money. I'll tell my MP so at his next surgery.'

By comparison the neat man appeared totally unconcerned. When he replied to the ill-tempered woman his voice, as usual, was quiet and calm.

'With respect, it wasn't the judge who turned you down. It was the defendant in the prisoner's dock.'

The revelation that it was the accused who'd rejected her and not someone in authority had the effect of adding to her sense of outrage.

'It says a lot for British justice when English people can be turned down in favour of an Asian and an ethnic. It's small wonder juries bring in cock-eyed verdicts!'

The man was unaffected by her outburst and quietly put her down.

'I'm sure both men will discharge their duty with as much integrity and diligence as the others.'

I was reminded of his remarks to the black youth about the privilege of serving as a juror and for the first time since we'd assembled in the jurors room it prompted me to comment.

'The young man from Brixton looked amazed there was no objection when he took the oath. I suspect he was even more so when you were turned down. I must admit I too was astonished at both decisions.'

He ignored my compliment. Instead he concentrated on the paradoxical selection.

'There was no question the man in the dock was shrewd. He assumed the black youth had no respect for authority, while on the other hand he saw me as traditionally establishment.

They were both sound reasons for his decisions to accept one and reject the other.'

Unconvinced and unappreciative, the woman made no attempt to hide her disapproval.

'If the accused man is so clever and cunning, why didn't he object to the Indian with the turban?'

It seemed as if the man had anticipated her question.

'He probably calculated the man would be even more sympathetic to him than the others.'

I was intrigued by his reply.

'More sympathetic? Why would he think that?'

'Because the Sikh, like the young black, has little regard for authority. It might be due to experience of the sort of attitudes we heard expressed in this room earlier on or it may be for purely psychological reasons.'

'Purely psychological reasons?'

'A subconscious resentment for the way the English kept law and order in India during the days of the British Raj. Innate and latent it might be, but a canny defendant would take it into account.'

The woman was in no mood for psycho-analytical reasoning.

'Rubbish! Anyway, it's got to be wrong bringing 20 people together when only 12 are wanted then sending eight back home without so much as a thank you. The system's a complete waste of time and taxpayers' money. And come to that, what right has a criminal to decide who sits on a jury to try him?'

The others who'd remained silent throughout the exchanges nodded agreement. As before, they left it to the man in the suit to explain the situation and he was willing to comply.

'The defendant in the dock may not be a criminal. But even if he is, he still has the right to challenge those he sees as likely to deny him a fair trial. The truth is any one of us may be prejudiced in their outlook even without recognising or acknowledging it.'

The expression on the woman's face indicated how profoundly she disagreed and took his remarks personally. She shook her shoulders like a bird settling feathers.

'There's nothing wrong with prejudice so long as it's on the side of justice. Villains aren't the only ones with rights. Law-abiding citizens have them too. In my opinion there'd be less crime in society if people with common sense had more to do with the legal system.' She squinted at him with narrowed eyes. 'You're not by any chance a lawyer?'

From his reaction it was impossible to gather if he was dismayed or flattered by her query.

'For your information, professional people are exempt from serving on a jury. So are priests. Jurors have to be lay persons. The whole purpose is to allow them to exercise their common sense in coming to judgements.'

I found the scope of his reasoning very impressive and couldn't resist making a personal observation.

'Listening to you now and even before we went into the courtroom to be sworn in, I must admit I saw you as perfect juror. More than that perhaps – an ideal foreman. Everything about you lays claim to that distinction. I'm sure when it came to the moment of rejection you must have felt deeply resentful at not being chosen?'

His face remained expressionless and when he replied his voice was without a trace of emotion.

'Deeply resentful? Not at all. I'm inured to it.'

His baffling response made the short-tempered woman more irritated than before.

'What do you mean inured to it?!'

'Because today isn't the first occasion I've been summoned for jury service.'

'Not the first occasion?' The woman and I spoke together.

'It's my third appearance and so far I've not once been selected.' As before, he was ready to go into detail. 'Contrary to general belief, there's no limit to how often you can be called to serve on a jury – that is, up to 65. Presumably the authorities consider old-age pensioners no longer capable of making reasoned judgements or staying the course of a long trial.'

There was a murmur of dismay from the rest of the group, but before anyone could comment and question him further the usher returned to the waiting room. As usual, she was briskly efficient.

'The jury's been sworn in and the judge has excused the rest of you further attendance. You're all free to go and claim your expenses from the pay office. It's down the corridor on the left.'

With that curt statement she departed. Not for the first time that morning I thought how effective a jury would be made up of 12 experienced officials like her instead of the randomly selected group such as ourselves. As the others made their way to the pay office the man in the suit and I remained seated. I wanted to acknowledge the rapport I felt existed between us. I waited till I was certain the others were out of hearing.

'I couldn't help but admire the way you responded to the woman with glasses when you explained why you'd been rejected from the panel. I fully expected her to challenge you for the reasons of her own dismissal.'

As always when he replied to a question, his voice was calm and his point of view objective.

'My opinion for her rejection would have made no impact. The lady's mind is set on every subject.'

I was keen to demonstrate that like him I was open-minded about the matter of rejection, even to the extent of defending the prickly woman.

'In fairness, was she really so unacceptable as a juror?'

His look could only be described as quizzical.

'If you were on trial and your freedom depended on the outcome, how would you view her sitting on the jury?'

'Certainly with mixed feelings but that's because I've had the opportunity of hearing her opinions and judging her character. I must say, the way you dealt with her prejudiced views, I could see you as the defendant's defence counsel in wig and gown.'

He inclined his head to acknowledge the compliment, then changing the subject gave me a searching glance.

'Weren't you at all interested to know why I considered the man in the dock gave you the thumbs down?'

I shrugged to appear quite unaffected by the decision.

'Let's say I was momentarily surprised. But nowhere near as shocked as when you followed me back here. Of us all I considered you the person most likely to be chosen as a juror. As I said to you before, in my opinion you'd have made an ideal foreman of the jury.'

He deliberately ignored my compliment and repeated his original question.

'You hadn't more than a moment's surprise when the man sent you packing? Not a moment's curiosity as to why?'

I could tell he was as keen to provide an explanation for my deselection as he'd been ready to explain his own.

'Very well. Why do you think he turned me down?'

'He turned you down because he saw you as standing against his own best interests.' His reply was made with the aplomb of a behavioural psychologist. 'It was a foregone conclusion. I could have predicted it.'

I could feel my eyebrows creating wrinkles on my forehead.

'A foregone conclusion?'

'He wasn't going to take a chance on someone dressed in a blazer with a regimental badge on its breast pocket.'

I stared dumbfounded. It never occurred to me I'd be categorised just as the wing-glassed woman had been with her biased views of class and race, simply by my clothes. I was rattled and felt obliged to justify my appearance.

'I didn't think being neatly dressed would classify me as one type of objectionable individual or another.'

He was indifferent to my hurt and prepared to add to it.

'I assure you the defendant felt that coming to court dressed as you are was done more so out of respect and consideration for the judge and his court than for him on the wrong side of the law.'

I was offended by the suggestion that it was social snobbery and deference to authority that made me dress as I did.

'For the record, I didn't consider coming in a T-shirt and trainers quite in keeping with the occasion.'

He ignored my sarcasm.

'Had you come like that, the man in the dock would have seen you as someone unimpressed by the pomp and circumstance of the law, an independently minded free spirit. Far from rejecting you, he'd have endorsed you. Dressed as you are, he wouldn't have picked you at any price!'

I took his remarks as not only being the defendant's view of me as a potentially hostile juror but also reflecting his own assessment of my type and character. I reacted defensively and with a critical observation of my own.

'The man in the dock might have given me the benefit of doubt. When all's said and done, a blazer, even one with a badge on the breast pocket, isn't as establishment as a pinstriped suit and old school tie.'

He paused several seconds before replying. For the first time in our brief conversation I sensed a subtle change in his manner. Gone was the bland objective point of view and calm impassive expression. There was even a faint twitch of a smile at the corners of his mouth. When he spoke his voice sounded more personal and sympathetic.

'You're absolutely right. My suit and tie are the reasons the man in the dock turned me down in favour of the sloven in the T-shirt and the young man with dreadlocks. But while you dressed to present yourself as an upright unbiased citizen prepared to do your civic duty and give him an honest trial regardless of any incriminating circumstances, I came to court today dressed as I am for exactly the opposite reasons!'

He paused in anticipation of my startled reply.

'Exactly opposite reasons?'

'A deliberate tactic.'

I waited, unsure if he was being facetious.

'I came dressed so blatantly establishment that it would guarantee my being rejected as a potential juror!'

He took no notice of my shocked look and head shaking with disbelief but went on to rationalise his actions.

'As I mentioned to you and the voluble lady a while ago, this is my third summons and after today's rejection there could well be a fourth. The system is foolproof but for that one drawback. However, the inconvenience of a morning's session lasting an hour or so has to be set against the boredom of sitting through a long trial with 11 other jurors who at the end of the day, as the lady with the ornate spectacles put it, are just as likely to bring in a perverse verdict as a correct one.'

The man's unblushing account for his deliberate deselection came as a profound shock and disappointment. Somehow by his deceitful actions the whole concept of a person being innocent of any charge till proven guilty by 12 honest and true peer citizens seemed a hollow mockery when such an able and intelligent man could deliberately disqualify himself from the legal process.

As we followed the others to the pay office, and later as we walked towards the Bank of England, in comparison to the morning's events everything seemed a depressing anti-climax. I was silent with disappointment at his cunning deception. At the entrance to the underground station he turned to me. He appeared without remorse or awareness of my feelings towards him. When he spoke he remained as calm and expressionless as he had done since we first met.

'Of course, there's no certainty you'll be picked from the hat a second time. Your electoral register may have so many names to choose from you could reach retirement and no longer be eligible. But just in case it happens and the timing doesn't happen to fit in with your routine, you might give some thought to my advice and experience.'

The remark was an unexpected invitation to express my true feelings, but I decided to reaffirm my sense of responsibility and civic duty rather than criticise his selfish and devious behaviour. I assumed a voice as bland and unemotional as his own.

'If as you say, dressed as I am, I appear an establishment

figure, so be it. I've no wish to give anyone, including defendants in the dock, any other impression. They see the person I am and must judge me accordingly. I have absolutely no desire to act out of character.'

When he nodded I wasn't sure if it was in recognition of my sterling qualities or regret for my innate naivety. He smoothed the fabric of his neatly wound umbrella and tapped a tattoo with it on the pavement. The military-style gesture was ostentatiously that of an ex-officer.

'I hear what you say about your reaction to the possibility of another summons ordering you to court. All I can remark is if you are faced with a repeat performance and you come dressed as you are today – a typical middle-class hip-hip-hooray – you can be quite certain of rejection a second time round. However, if sitting through weeks of boring legal arguments appeals to you as the most stimulating way of spending your leisure time then I suggest that for the first time in your life you act out of character and come dressed in a grubby T-shirt and dirty trainers. The judge will look down his nose at you from the bench with undisguised disapproval but the unfortunate person in the dock will give you the proverbial thumbs up.'

He paused at the top of the stairs. There was the trace of a wistful expression on his face.

'I tell you this for what it's worth. If at some future time you are elected to a jury, I have no doubt the other 11 jurors empaneled with you will immediately recognise your superior intellect and social standing and defer to your opinions. At the end of the day, in their collective view – and for what it's worth in mine as well – you'd make an absolutely ideal foreman.'

With that he shouldered arms with his umbrella and disappeared down the Bank of England underground.

THE SUMMING UP

Justice Pelham-Brooke sat in the Old Bailey courtroom, calm and inscrutable. A shaft of dust-filled sunlight streamed through the high windows and pierced the 12 jurors ranked on their wooden benches. Up in the visitors' gallery a handful of spectators looked down on the scene – the judge in his high-backed chair authoritative and resplendent in ermine cloak and purple sash, and below, in the well of the court, counsels for the prosecution and defence sitting side by side with their juniors grouped behind and all dressed in identical wigs and gowns. One row further back, solicitors and clerks scribbled in their notebooks while court ushers stood at strategic points ready to convey messages and exhibits as directed. All 12 members of the jury wore expressions of intense concentration as the barrister for the prosecution rose to make his final speech in a week-long trial nearing its climax.

'Milord, ladies and gentlemen of the jury.'

He stood silently scanning the jurors, both arms bent at the elbow and hands grasping the folds of his black silk gown. The deliberate pause and theatrical pose had the mannerisms of an actor about to make the most of an opportunity to impact on a rapt and captive audience in the closing moments of a melodramatic play.

'During the proceedings of this trial you have been presented with evidence for and against the accused man in the dock charged with murder. Witnesses have appeared before you to give personal accounts of incidents leading up to the tragic event, as have medical and forensic specialists been called to offer their professional conclusions. You have also heard from the accused himself, giving his own account of the final moments in this tragic affair. Now we are at the closing stages of this murder trial, when my learned friend, for the defence, and I, on behalf of the Crown, present our final arguments for and against the defendant. When we are both done, his honour, the judge, will review the case and comment on those aspects of the law as they apply to this highly unusual case. It will without doubt be wise and impartial guidance, but in the final analysis, when all is said and done, it will then be up to you, members of the jury, to decide whether or not the accused is guilty of the crime with which he is charged.'

At this reminder of their personal responsibilities, one way or another all 12 jurors made as if to emphasise their awareness of the gravity of the situation and of their unreserved commitment to perform their civic duty. Several hunched forward in their seats while others sat back and folded their arms across their chests. All assumed expressions of profound concentration. For his part, Judge Pelham-Brooke's face was emotionless as he listened to the prosecutor's familiar preamble which reminded him of so many other murder trials over which he'd presided during his long and distinguished career. Quite suddenly, the tone of the barrister's voice changed. For his opening remarks it had been emotionless and objective, now it was sharp-edged and menacing. With a withering glance in the direction of the drawn-faced figure sitting flanked by warders in the prisoner's dock, he pointed a stabbing accusative finger towards him.

'You have heard it claimed by the defendant speaking in defence of his actions, that in a long and fraught marriage he suffered continual provocation from a vindictive and quarrelsome wife, that it was as a result of an outpouring of personal abuse and demeaning insults that the final fateful incident took place; an incident which has brought him to trial in this criminal courtroom for you to judge whether or not he is guilty of the grisly crime with which he is charged, which the prosecution maintains he is, or if there were any mitigating circumstances to take into account for his wife's violent death as counsel for defence claims.'

Although the jurors had heard the case explained in minute and repetitive detail throughout the trial and made copious notes of the relevant facts, nevertheless, at the behest of the QC, they stared back at him as if to indicate that by hearing the catalogue of events once again they'd be even more certain of coming to a correct and just decision. At the same time as they sat focused on the prosecutor's belligerent manner and strident tone, Pelham-Brooke mused on the sense of unreality and remoteness of the proceedings being enacted before him. In a career spanning 20 years on the bench, first as a magistrate, then as a recorder and finally a judge in Crown Courts, he'd frequently presided over cases of domestic violence which all too often had ended with tragic consequences. As he sat listening to the prosecuting counsel he was struck by the remoteness of a criminal court in dealing with events that only the accused and the victim could know and verify; that no matter how well intentioned and objective the judicial effort, it was impossible to ever know for certain the absolute truth of what went on between the two people concerned. And to compound that anomalous situation, for 12 lay citizens, randomly assembled, to come to an objective and reasoned decision of the defendant's guilt or innocence. But for him personally, the most dramatic element in any murder trial was the presiding judge's review of the case and his final summing up at the end, all of which was to be delivered with total impartiality, striving with legal nicety to avoid influencing the jury in coming to a just and independent decision. And if, when they'd concluded their deliberations, they found the accused guilty as charged, to impose the only sentence permissible by law – imprisonment for life. Once again the prosecuting counsel's grating voice broke into Pelham-Brooke's reflective thoughts.

'Uncontested and unarguable facts made by impartial witnesses are what you have to consider in your deliberations. For example, the evidence of police called to the scene of the crime and the pathologist who carried out the post-mortem on the body – all of whom originally reported their findings to the coroner at the inquest on the dead woman and whose court declared the victim had not died accidentally. You have even heard from the defendant himself when relating his account of events that took place on the fateful day his wife died, that it was as a consequence of her provocation over intimate personal details – the nature of which have no bearing on the case – and that it was as a result of her spiteful taunts that in a sudden burst of uncontrollable rage he grasped her round the neck with both hands and shook her so violently that as a result she suffered fatal spinal injuries and died within a few seconds from its vicious effects.'

Again the QC assumed a theatrical stance as he silently held both arms at full length and with claw-like hands simulated the severe shaking action he'd just described in clinical detail. He remained silent for several seconds, scrutinising each juror in turn as if to assess the personal effect his graphic demonstration had on them.

'No doubt the fact will have already occurred to you that the defence makes no challenge to the circumstances that caused the woman's death, only the interpretation the Crown puts on it. It is to resolve that difference of interpretation between us that the prosecution has to put this question to you: what motive can we ascribe to a man who by his own account was involved in nothing more serious than a domestic dispute but who nevertheless resorted to extreme physical violence to end it? It is our contention that the violent action carried out by a man with his normal strength increased by venomous rage made that violent assault on his defenceless wife with the intention not to temporarily still her nagging tongue but silence it forever. If, as the defence claims, the action was simply to still her abusive tongue and was made without any evil intent, is it reasonable to accept that the accused grasped his wife by the throat with both hands and squeezed with such strength that her spinal cord was severed? That the action was a momentary aberration on the defendant's part totally at variance with his normal calm and rationally controlled behaviour? That the tragedy arising from his impulsive action was an accident and not deliberate?'

Again he silently scanned the jurors' faces to gauge their reactions.

'When called upon to give evidence, medical and forensic experts stated that in their view clasping the neck with both hands and squeezing was not an action designed to inflict minor discomfort or result in personal humiliation. To achieve that effect a slap with the open hand to the side of the face would be more usual and appropriate. In this case the physical action was of a man sloughing off his responsibilities to his wife of 25 years and made for no other purpose than to kill her! It was the response of a man out of control of mind and body. Remember, an act of violence which ends a human life does not have to be premeditated, it can be spontaneous as it was in this macabre case. At the end of the day it is for you the jury to decide whether the fatal action carried out by the defendant against his wife was accidental or deliberate. Taking every factor into account, the prosecution claims that on the evidence put before this court and as responsible citizens – each and every one of you carrying out your civic duty to the best of your ability – there is only one conclusion you can come to, only one verdict you can return. That in the final analysis you are bound to find the accused guilty of murder!'

As the prosecuting counsel draped his gown around him and sat down, the eyes of the jurors turned from him and searched the face of the figure in the dock as if to glean some fresh understanding of the events of that fateful day. And as they sat and stared, Pelham-Brooke's legal mind assumed control over his thoughts and busied himself with the form of a speech that would guide the 12 jurors in the difficult task facing them when they retired to make their final decision. Who among them, he would emphasise, required to pass judgement on a fellow man could search their minds and hearts and say that at some time in their lives they hadn't been provoked beyond control? And how tragic that loss of control could have been if it resulted in another person's death. This element of human vulnerability was to be made calmly and objectively so as to firm any wavering thoughts and reinforce reasoned conclusions. An accused man's freedom was at stake – his life maybe. The responsibilities were heavy upon each and every one of them.

During this silent rehearsal the judge sat motionless and expressionless, momentarily lost in reflective thought. Only the quietly sympathetic voice of counsel for defence interrupted his silent reverie and brought him back to the reality of the courtroom trial.

'Milord, ladies and gentlemen of the jury.'

Adopting the same gown-clasping stance as that of his fellow barrister but in contrast to his professional opponent's aggressive manner, the defending QC adopted an air of profound sympathy and deepest understanding. When he spoke his voice was resonant with compassion.

'Here is a case where one could in all humility put a hand to one's heart and say: "There but for the grace of God, go I."'

He paused, as if reflecting on all human frailty, including that of his own, and briefly looked from the jury to the defendant in the dock.

'I wonder if at some time during the course of this heart-rending case the thought has occurred to each of you that although the circumstances of this bizarre case make it exceptional, in many ways they are a reminder that the tragic incidents which have befallen the defendant and brought him to trial in this courtroom might, if the fates so conspired, treat any one of us in a similar fashion. That at the end of the day we are all accountable for our daily actions and vulnerable with regard to the impersonal law!'

He glanced to his opponent QC sitting relaxed and neutral by his side.

'Throughout this sad and harrowing trial, my learned friend, the Crown prosecutor, repeatedly described the defendant as a man of savage and aggressive temperament. To add to that description of a flawed and dangerous personality, in his final address he also demonstrated with elaborate gestures the violent throttling action the accused used against his wife, simulating the shaking of her by the neck, thereby causing her death. As each and every one of us can testify from personal experience, the human body is the frailest of structures, frequently susceptible during the course of mundane day-to-day circumstances to a variety of injuries. At no time during this week's hearing has the defence disputed the forensic evidence as to the cause of the woman's death, nor does it so now. But to agree the physical causes of the defendant's wife's broken spine is in no way to admit or imply that those fatal injuries were deliberately and maliciously inflicted. On the contrary, as he swore on oath when giving his version of events that tragic day, the accused did not appreciate a momentary shaking of his wife's neck could result in her death. The outcome of his entirely reflexive action was beyond his wildest imagination or logical comprehension. It was simply the fleeting response of a man goaded beyond his normal limit of control.'

Once more the defending barrister stood glancing around the courtroom, casting his eyes first at the judge sitting impassively in his high-backed chair, then to the prosecuting counsel and finally from him to the jurors.

'I started this final appeal to you by quoting a famously familiar saying. The remark, "There but for the grace of God, go I", was made by a man standing by a public gallows not more than a mile or two from this very courtroom. As he watched a man hanged for a petty crime he reflected on the law's cruel arbitrariness and how under certain circumstances it might equally apply to his own human failings and infidelities. Four hundred years later I put the same soul-searching reflection to you and ask who among us at some time in their lives has not been involved in situations which stir us to such an extent that momentarily we lose control over our emotions? Such confrontations may occur in different places but most frequently are within our own homes and between those nearest and dearest to us. It is there that inflamed passions are aroused and result in extremes of human behaviour.'

He gestured towards the defendant sitting pale and tense in the dock.

'This is what happened to the man on trial before you that fateful day – a day that for the most part was as uneventful as any other in his regular and responsible routine. During the course of the trial you have been told of the tensions that culminated in the quarrel between the defendant and his wife. By now those details must be firmly implanted in your minds. I would instead remind you that the reporting of her accidental death was freely given by the defendant to the police. In no way were the facts of that humiliating and ultimately fatal confrontation dissembled or his actions excused. It was a statement volunteered by a man of conscience and integrity. A man regarded by contemporaries as a person of the highest worth and scrupulous probity. A man who, up to the fateful event that brought him to this court of justice, held high and responsible office in his dedicated service to society.'

Yet again he paused to regard the jurors, now concentrating as intensely on his comments as they had to the Crown prosecutor's closing speech.

'My learned friend in his closing speech made the same observation about the defendant's illustrious background. He too considered those intimate details to have a direct and profound bearing on the issue before you. But the details were mentioned less to enlist your sympathy than to portray the accused as a man who while appearing to be a character of worth and achievement in his public life was also capable of perverse and cruel behaviour in his private life. It was Crown counsel's purpose to present the defendant as a modern-day Jekyll and Hyde in the hope that by so doing he would influence your judgement and for you to find the accused guilty of the crime with which he is charged.'

From his special vantage point in the courtroom, Andrew Pelham-Brooke glanced at the faces of the jurors, who were transfixed by the defence barrister's impassioned contention that everything rested upon their acceptance of the defendant's version of events. With half-closed eyes he concentrated on the evidence highlighted throughout the trial. Of references to the wife's malicious and venomous disposition and the placid husband's temper fanned by personal abuse and the lapse of control as he shook her in an unconsciously violent action that ended in her death from a broken neck. A man's life or freedom rested upon the acceptance or otherwise that the jury placed on the accused's account of that fateful quarrel. Accidental death or deliberate murder? How could they know? Once again his thoughts were interrupted by counsel as he made his closing remarks.

'Ladies and gentlemen of the jury.' The QC slowly scanned each juror's face in turn. 'When you retire to consider your verdict, it is in no sense of the word an exaggeration to claim that the scales of justice will be held in your hands. Each of you will have to decide whether through the most bizarre and unpredictable of circumstances the statements of an honourable man accountable to this court and the law of the land are true. On oath he has related events that led to a devastating climactic episode in an otherwise ordered and blameless life. On oath he has stated the death of his wife was a tragic accident, that the impulsive reflexive action he took to still the abuse being heaped on him by a vitriolic wife only resulted in her death through an abnormal physical condition which neither he nor anyone could have predicted. For him to be found guilty of murder and incarcerated for life imprisonment would not only be the gravest miscarriage of justice but a heinous and inhumane decision. It is one of the great traditions of English law that a person accused of a crime be given the benefit of any doubt that exists in their case. The defence now appeals to you to exercise that prerogative. Upon your acceptance of the defendant's admission of having accidentally caused his wife's death depends his entire future. That in the final analysis your unanimous verdict will be not guilty!'

When the defence counsel resumed his seat there was a tense silence. Listening to the QC's closing speech, Andrew Pelham-Brooke sat composed and impassive as he had done throughout the trial. All that remained in these dramatic proceedings was the judge's review and summary of the facts for the guidance of the jury. He was well aware of the daunting task ahead and assumed an air of anxious expectancy. For the first time in the week-long trial the eyes of the scarlet-robed figure on the bench met those of the prisoner in the dock. In a slow and measured voice the judge spoke the opening lines that marked his summing up of the case of the Crown versus the accused – on trial for the murder of his wife, Hester Pelham-Brooke.

MISTER NOBODY

Oliver W. Trotter OBE had a recurring nightmare. His entire family were gathered at the foot of his bed gloomily staring at him lying paralysed and speechless from a crippling stroke and waiting for him to die. He wanted to reassure them he was in no physical discomfort or mental stress and that at 70 years of age, having led a full life, he was quite content to leave it, but try as he might the words wouldn't come. Then the scene changed and he was standing in an atmosphere that was bright and sunny with wispy clouds floating in an azure sky. Sitting behind a desk studying a ledger was a patriarchal figure. His hair and beard were as white as the flowing robe that covered his body from neck to ankle. There was no doubting he was St. Peter and the location the pearly gates to Heaven.

As the archangel moved his finger on the open pages, the expression on his face was stern and occasionally his head shook from side to side as if some particular entry caused him concern. The reading went on for some minutes, and Trotter, miffed at being ignored, shuffled and coughed discreetly. The archangel still took no notice and continued studying the thick-paged tome. Then at last he looked up.

'Oliver W. Trotter?'

'Yes.'

'What does "W" stand for?'

'Wilbur.'

There was the trace of a smile on the angel's face.

'I'm not surprised you used the initial "W".'

As the archangel went back to perusing the book, Trotter glanced around him as if searching for something in particular.

It was minutes more before he plucked up the courage to speak again.

'I know the description's purely figurative, but I assume I'm at the pearly gates; that I'm about to enter Heaven?'

St. Peter continued reading but didn't bother to look up.

'You're right in the first part but not the second.'

Trotter stared in surprise.

'Not the second? But surely this is the entrance to Heaven?'

The archangel leaned back in his chair, 'Not the entrance to Heaven, singular – the entrance to heavens, plural!'

'Plural?!'

There was a strained look on his face.

'Why do you look so surprised? On Earth you were quite fond of exclaiming heavens above; that is, whenever the expression suited your purpose.'

'But it was just an expression. I didn't actually believe it.'

St. Peter was irritated.

'Oh I know that! I know exactly what you did and didn't believe. Well, to coin another phrase you were fond of using, there's many a true word spoken in jest. As you so ignorantly and unimaginatively put it, there really are heavens above.'

He ignored Trotter's look of uncomprehending disbelief.

'Would it be right to put the good with the excellent and the exemplary with the noble? Would it be fitting to lump them all together? Would it be celestial justice?' There was no pause for a response as he continued. 'Harmony is only achieved up here by allocating angels to an appropriate heaven. Putting them all together in one open-plan establishment would be chaotic. As a former methodical man yourself, you surely appreciate that?'

Trotter realised the question was rhetorical but brightened considerably.

'I must be honest, St. Peter, I never imagined there being different grades of angels, but now you've explained it, the administrative arrangements do seem logical.' He beamed contentedly. 'Still, it's gratifying to know I'm due to be allocated to one of Heaven's heavens.'

The archangel didn't reply. Instead he looked again at the book on his desk and riffled the pages, scanning each perfunctorily with a frown on his face. When at last he spoke, his voice was cold.

'I've been going through your record, Oliver W. Trotter, and I have to tell you that judged by our standards your life on Earth didn't amount to very much.'

For several seconds, Trotter was speechless. Then he reacted, stung to the quick.

'What do you mean my life on Earth didn't amount to very much?'

'Just what I say.'

St. Peter held the ledger in his hands.

'To use an analogy and compare it to a company balance sheet, your liabilities more than outweigh your assets. In fact, there are several entries which take you close to bankruptcy. Translated into spiritual jargon, that's eternal damnation!'

Trotter's eyes bulged and his limbs trembled.

'Eternal damnation? I take it you're speaking metaphorically?'

The archangel's brows knitted and his voice was low and gruff.

'We don't use metaphors here. When we say eternal damnation we mean the nether region. What you as an Earthling referred to as Hell.'

The word struck such terror into Trotter that involuntarily

he shut his eyes as if to blank out a fearful image. Then in a swift bold show of aggression he stepped forward to the desk.

'I didn't lead the kind of life that warrants my going to Hell. I'm not claiming I was blameless but compared to many others I knew, I'd say I was above average.'

'Above average? Really!'

St. Peter's sarcastic tone spurred Trotter to further self-justification. He spoke urgently, breathlessly, as he pointed to the tome.

'It's all in there! I was a senior civil servant in Whitehall, and Borough Councillor for my local authority. As a result of these combined civic duties I was awarded an OBE from Her Majesty the Queen at Buckingham Palace. Moreover, I was a faithful husband and dutiful father. I never swore at any of my offspring or raised my hands in temper even when sorely provoked. I was never drunk in public nor did I ever deliberately break the law. In other words, I was in all regards a model citizen. On that basis and using your terminology as an example, I consider my credits far outweigh my debits and never for a moment was I near to being a moral bankrupt. I don't claim I'm entitled to enter Heaven with the exemplary, the excellent or the noble, but I certainly feel I qualify for the merely good.'

The archangel listened silently to Trotter's impassioned outburst, only drumming his fingers impatiently on the cover of the book. When finally he spoke, his voice was low and serious.

'Did you believe in God?'

Momentarily, Trotter was embarrassed and looked uncomfortable.

'As an agnostic I gave serious thought to there being

an Almighty. I discussed the subject more frequently with religious contemporaries than they did among themselves, particularly on those occasions when we met in church or chapel.'

St. Peter was scornful and dismissive.

'Those particular occasions count for nothing as far as we're concerned. Most people react to a holy atmosphere. Feeling pious because you're all dressed up for a wedding or a funeral is merely a combination of guilt and superstition, not faith.'

Trotter was dejected at the counter-attack and his voice dropped to a low whine.

'The 20th century wasn't the best of times to feel religious. What with men landing on the Moon and shuttling back and forth in space. It seemed mankind was finding out all there was to know about the universe; that scientists were able to perform even greater miracles than were in the Bible. You appreciate that to an enquiring layman like myself they did seem to make God redundant?'

Rather than being impressed, the archangel became more brusquely dismissive.

'An enquiring layman like yourself may have thought science had answers to the universe but did you ever enquire who may actually have been responsible for those scientists and their postbiblical miracles?'

Trotter's mien was defensive with embarrassment.

'It was a question of priorities. There were many claims made on me for most of my lifetime, what with a demanding career in Whitehall and a fraught domestic situation in Weybridge. It really was only after retirement and my family had all left home that I had time to reflect on religion per se.'

St. Peter's body bristled and his eyes flashed angrily.

'Oh, we know when you found the time to reflect per se! It was when you had a paralysing stroke and thought you were about to die!'

The accusation caused Trotter to sound ever more plaintive.

'Isn't it natural to wonder if there's a hereafter when you think you're going to leave the present? It doesn't seems unreasonable to me.'

'It may not seem unreasonable to you as a previously committed agnostic, but it's totally unacceptable for your late conversion to religion to count with us.' He suddenly rose from his chair. 'Really! The way you mortals come up here with your explanations and excuses. As if you were the arbiters of morals and beliefs and not God Almighty. Well, let me tell you, it wouldn't have mattered to us if you'd been less dedicated as a senior civil servant or conscientious as a borough councillor. We'll leave the question of the Queen's medal and marital fidelity on the credit side. But the fact remains, as far as Heaven's concerned you could have led a better life than you did – much better.'

At this onslaught, Trotter changed from cringing self-righteousness to abject appeal.

'If only I'd had some sort of sign when I was alive and well. Like a divine visitation or a heavenly voice. I would have been better than I was – much better!'

The archangel's lips curled derisively.

'If only! If only! That's the excuse I get all the time. Considering you were on Earth for 70 years, there were plenty of opportunities if you'd wanted to take advantage of them. You didn't have to believe everything that was written in the Old or New Testament but you could have taken the main principle on board. That wasn't too much to ask for, was it?'

St. Peter closed the book and placed it to one side of the desk.

'Well, that's it then!'

Trotter looked forlorn. He waited several seconds.

'What do you mean, "that's it then"?'

'I mean it's too late to be sorry that you weren't better than you were.'

'Too late to be sorry? Too late for what?'

'Too late to qualify for Heaven.'

Trotter stared at St. Peter in absolute disbelief. Then with the fury of a man unjustly accused and cruelly sentenced, his voice rose high in protest.

'All the time I've stood here I've had the feeling you were prejudiced against me, that you regarded me as some sort of earthly neuter. You said that though my life wasn't actually bad it wasn't particularly good and that nothing of what I achieved counted in my favour. As far as you were concerned I was a non-person, a nobody. Never once did you give the impression I might be considered a borderline case and let into Heaven. Well, I don't accept your judgement. I wish to appeal against your decision.'

For the first time since the interview began, St. Peter lost his composure. He got up, moved to the front of his desk and stood glowering.

'You're not at a borough council meeting up here you know. There is no appeal against this chairman's decision. As far as I'm concerned the interview is over.'

Trotter was distraught.

'What do you mean the interview's over? If you're refusing me entry into Heaven, where else is there for me to go?'

'The only place you can go. To the nether region, to Hell!

Now be off with you.'

The abrupt dismissal had the opposite effect. Trotter folded his arms across his chest in a flamboyant gesture of defiance.

'I had no intention of going to Hell when I was alive and I see no justification for you sending me there now. You said the Almighty's responsible for everything that goes on in the universe. Well, he alone should decide who qualifies for Heaven, not you. I want him to review my case. I want to speak to God!'

For a moment, St. Peter seemed affected by the impassioned outburst. He nodded and stroked his beard and when he spoke there was a note of sadness in his voice.

'What a pity you didn't display such a passion for Heaven while you were on Earth. It would have tipped the scales in your favour. As it is, I'm afraid you've left your conversion too late.'

Trotter assumed the attitude and voice of a petulant child.

'Well I won't go to Hell and you can't make me. I'll jolly well stay here till you see reason and change your mind.'

'Is that a fact now?'

It was with surprising agility that St. Peter stooped down and pulled the cloud Trotter was standing on so that he lost his balance and jerked backwards. The last he saw of the blue skies of Heaven as he tumbled into space was of St. Peter throwing the book after him and calling out in a fading voice.

'Goodbye and good riddance, Oliver Wilbur Trotter OBE. Mister Nobody!'

He sped head over heels through the atmosphere and passed his family still standing sombrely by his bedside. He knew for certain they'd heard him because of their long faces and tearful eyes, mistakenly believing they'd heard his dying gasp.

He continued down through stygian darkness till he landed on his feet in a dimly lit room. It was several seconds before he could adjust his vision to see clearly through the hazy atmosphere. Sitting behind a desk was a creature with horns protruding from his temples and legs ending in cloven hooves. Like his counterpart in Heaven, he was seated behind a large desk reading a book. For several minutes he turned the pages without once glancing up to acknowledge Trotter's arrival. Occasionally he pulled at his goatee beard and tutted as if disapproving of some entry or other in the ledger.

Trotter was in no doubt where he was nor whose record the demon was studying. In spite of the sauna-like humidity he felt shivery and was filled with apprehension. Although he'd shown impatience at being kept waiting at the pearly gates, he was more inhibited to attract attention in front of this Mephistophelean interviewer. After a while the demon closed the book and looked up. In spite of his animal-like appendages, the overall effect was not inhuman and unlike the stern-faced archangel in Heaven his expression was genial and his tone friendly.

'Oliver W. Trotter?'

He didn't wait for an acknowledgement.

'What does the "W" stand for?'

'Wilbur! I was named after my grandfather.'

There was a twinkle in his eyes as he repeated the name.

'Wilbur. That's late Victorian. A good period as far as we were concerned.'

Without enlarging upon the subject, he pointed to the book on his desk.

'Well, Oliver Wilbur Trotter OBE, I've been going through your record here and I'm afraid I have to tell you that it's not very good.'

At this unexpected and to him totally unjustified accusation, Oliver Trotter momentarily lost his self-control.

'Not very good? Not very good?! That's the second time today that remark's been said to me. Well, let me tell you, I didn't find it acceptable the first time it was made and I most certainly don't accept it now that it's repeated.'

The demon listened to the outburst with a blank expression and remained silent as Trotter continued his outburst.

'I'll tell you exactly the same as I told the other person about what's in that record. While it's true I had occasional lapses of behaviour and some unworthy thoughts when I was young, for most of my time as a human being I resisted temptations and made every effort to lead a decent, respectable life. I had no intention of going to Hell during my lifetime and now that I'm dead I haven't changed my mind. I have no wish to sound belligerent or ungrateful but as of this moment in time that's how I feel about the situation.'

He stood defiantly as if daring his interviewer to disagree. For his part, the demon listened to the speech without a change of expression. When after some deliberation he replied, his voice, in strong contrast to his devilish mien, was sympathetic.

'I understand your passionate reaction, Wilbur Trotter, I really do. But I must put you right on one vital issue. Contrary to your belief about the present situation, at this moment in time you are not yet in Hell – not in any one of them.'

Trotter's jaw gaped as if punched in the solar plexus. His voice too was strained.

'Not yet in Hell?'

The devil repeated calmly and patiently.

'Not in any one of them. You see, while we don't cater for

the same clientele as Heaven, we do nonetheless have features in common. For instance, like them, we in the nether region have more than one establishment.'

'More than one establishment? You're saying there's more than one hell?'

Trotter's air of incredulity provoked an impatient reaction.

'Naturally! You don't imagine we lump everyone together? Put the bad with the awful or monsters in with fiends?! Punishment has to fit the crime. Besides, what peace would there be down here if we didn't do that? Eternal damnation's one thing, eternal chaos another.'

The explanation had Trotter quaking and his voice quavering.

'You said just now that my record wasn't very good. Does that mean I might not just be put in with the bad or the awful, but with monsters – or even fiends?!'

The demon's beard hid his smiling lips but there was no concealing his amusement.

'I know it sounds paradoxical, Wilbur, but when I said your record wasn't very good, what I meant, as far as we down here are concerned, is that it really wasn't very bad.'

While Trotter stared speechless, the demon flicked through several pages of the book.

'Let me give you an example. Here, this entry under mid-life crisis. You were married to the same woman for 24 years, and father to her four children, when you got a crush on a colleague at the Ministry of Eggs and Fisheries where you were both Grade 2 civil servants. Then, when passion swamped your senses and you decided to spend three nights with her in Paris, you told your wife you'd been summoned to a conference on third world starvation. You then compounded the deceit by forging her signature on a joint bank account and withdrew £500 to pay for the illicit weekend. But on the rough crossing to France and feeling next to death's door, you had second thoughts about the clandestine affair and after agonising to your lover about fidelity and ethics decided to return home and tell your wife the conference was cancelled due to the Red Cross dropping food into the countries most affected. Then, at the first opportunity, you returned the stolen money and bought your wife an eternity ring as a silver wedding anniversary present.'

He sat back in his chair and assumed the manner of a professional analyst.

'Let's look at that incident in detail. You decide to be unfaithful to your wife with a colleague 15 years your junior – that's fine! You then forge your wife's signature for the sinful purpose – better still! Then when it comes to consummating the affair, you chicken out. Not as a result of post-coital depression because you never reached a climax, but you abandoned a thoroughly reprehensible action, which would have counted in your favour, simply because of conscience. Looked at objectively, that event was a sorry tale of physical cowardice and moral compromise. And it wasn't an isolated incident either. There were others of a comparable nature. The truth of the matter, Wilbur, is that you lived your life being neither one thing nor the other – a kind of neuter, a Mister Nobody. I'm sorry to have to put it this way, but from our point of view you're unsuitable for Hell. In other words, you're a nether region reject!'

Trotter stood transfixed. Then, like a valve released from dangerous pressure, gave vent to his anger.

'You've the gall to sit there and say I'm not good enough

for Hell? Me? A senior civil servant awarded the OBE by Her Majesty the Queen of England. A borough councillor who on occasions stood in for the chairman at mayoral functions. You can't be serious saying I'm a nether region reject? No way can that be fair!'

The demon was surprised by the aggressive response.

'Whether you think it fair or not, Wilbur, I'm afraid that's the case. You must appreciate that just as St. Peter is particular about who he admits to Heaven, so am I about who I let into Hell. Naturally, serial killers, rapists, paedophiles, corrupt politicians, decadent popstars and power-crazed tycoons automatically qualify, just as saints, martyrs, philanthropists and Vatican popes do for Heaven. I'm talking about applicants who've led neutral lives, who were nothing in particular and sent down here for an interview. In other words, I'm referring to the mass of ordinary people on Earth – the nobodies of the world.'

The résumé left Trotter struggling to come to terms with the concept of Heaven and Hell, both only catering for an exclusive elite.

'Are you saying you reject the majority who come down here?'

'The vast majority! We may be hosts to a multi-racial, multi-cultural society, but I assure you we're not overcrowded – not any more, I imagine, than Heaven above.'

The revelation left Trotter more bewildered than before. Instead of continuing to rage and protest, suddenly he was deflated and dejected.

'But if we're refused entry into Heaven and Hell, where do we ex-Earthlings go? Where do we stay? Presumably there has to be a place for reject spirits, otherwise what's the purpose of there being an afterlife?'

The demon leaned back in his chair. In spite of his horns and hooves he had the look of a philosophic sage.

'It's a good question, Wilbur, but I'm surprised you ask it of me. Born and bred Church of England as you were, though obviously never devout, you surely must have heard of being in limbo? Maybe even on occasions referred to it yourself?'

At the reminder of his religious shortcomings, Trotter looked embarrassed and shifted uneasily from foot to foot.

'There were times I may have used the expression but to be honest I didn't think it existed. I didn't think limbo was an actual place.'

There was an impish expression on the demon's face as if relishing the subject.

'If you'd been as inquisitive about Christianity as you were about other things you'd have known limbo was the area between Heaven and Hell. Even biblical prophets realised most human beings wouldn't live up to Jesus's standards, that they'd live lives being nothing in particular and as a result when they died would have to be accommodated somewhere in the universe. That's why they designated limbo. In strictly Earthling language, it's a spiritual no man's land.'

The explanation only added to Trotter's depression.

'You said before there had to be justice in Hell the same as anywhere else, but where's the justice in sending me to the middle of nowhere? Wandering around not being one thing or another – a nameless entity? That's a sentence of a most heartless kind.'

The demon leaned back in his chair and looked thoughtful.

'I understand your disappointment, Wilbur, I really do. Although being despatched to an atmospheric wilderness is routine procedure, I take on board the point you make about ending up a nameless entity. On the issue of anonymity, I'm inclined to agree that is pouring salt on wounds. While in the state of limbo, spirits should at least have an identity. In your case something to distinguish you as having been an earthly OBE – a title as distinctive as devil, or even angel.'

At this surprising comment, Trotter warmed to him with rekindled enthusiasm.

'I'm pleased you see it from my point of view. A title would offset the ignominy of being banished from both Heaven and Hell – of ending up nothing in particular. It would be an inspired compromise. It could well have come from St. Peter.'

The demon was flattered and looked at Trotter with a self-deprecatory expression.

'You understand that at short notice it's only a suggestion off the top of my head, but I think I have the answer. It's a sort of generic term that could well apply to other rejected spirits like yourself.'

He pointed to the book on his desk.

'For instance, going through this record it was obvious you were regarded by your contemporaries as someone of above average abilities and influence, particularly those responsible to you in the Ministry of Eggs and Fisheries. A big white chief. What ancient Indians reverentially referred to as a mugwump.'

Trotter beamed and nodded enthusiastically.

'At the same time you were also a man of a scientific disposition, unwilling to believe in things that couldn't be explained or proved to your satisfaction – pronouncements of a materialistic or miraculous nature in particular. You were what those with orthodox religious faith referred to as an agnostic.'

Again, Trotter silently acknowledged his agreement.

'Now, if we take those two dominant features of your character into account I suggest an appropriate title for an above average intellectual-cum-spiritual rebel such as yourself could very accurately be a "mugwostic"!' He leaned back in his chair, arms clasped behind his neck and a smug expression on his face. He repeated the word. 'Mugwostic! The name rolls off the tongue. I like it. It suits you.'

Instead of sharing the demon's enthusiasm, Trotter was glum and depressed.

'The way you described me as an intellectual-cum-spiritual rebel just because I was ambitious in my career and queried religious miracles wasn't just disappointing, it was hurtful. I didn't see either trait as character defects. I mean no disrespect, but not only does the term you've dreamed up seem inappropriate, it sounds like some sort of mongrel. It's nothing like as distinctive as angel or terrifying as devil. As far as I'm concerned, I'd rather be called a reject spirit than a mugwostic.'

The demon was hurt by the criticism and shifted irritably in his chair.

'I was only trying to be helpful and ease your way from here. I don't usually spend time discussing philosophy or making constructive suggestions with interviewees. Still, as you're not happy with my terminology, let's forget all about it.' With that he closed the book and held it out in front of him. 'Here. Take this with you. Keep it as a memento.'

Instinctively, Trotter backed away from the desk so that the book was out of reach.

'No! I won't take it. I've been wrongly assessed down here in Hell just as I was up in Heaven. I've been misunderstood and haven't been given any benefit of the doubt. I want to appeal against your decision. I want to speak to Satan!'

At mention of the name, a dull reddish glow suffused the smoky atmosphere and transformed it from benign to sinister. When the demon replied, all pleasantry was gone from his voice, which now sounded hollow and sepulchral.

'You can't speak to anyone. There is no appeal against my judgement.'

Trotter folded his arms across his chest and stood with his feet spread apart in an attitude of fearless defiance.

'Very well then, I won't go!'

With that the demon rose from his chair. Suddenly, there was nothing remotely human or philosophical about his appearance. His eyes pinpointed menacingly.

'You won't go? Really? Then we'll have to see.'

With that he puffed his cheeks and blew him from the desk. The last thing Trotter heard as he flew back up into the atmosphere was a faint mocking voice.

'Goodbye and good riddance, Mister Nobody!'

It was always at that precise moment in the dream that Oliver W. Trotter awoke, his heart pounding and body damp with sweat. The first thing he did was move his limbs to make sure he wasn't paralysed, then glance around the room to confirm there were no family relations at the bedside waiting for him to die. He then lay back on the pillow, staring up at the ceiling and reliving the familiar dream.

In the stillness of the dark night he wondered if his confrontations with St. Peter and the devil were subconscious warnings for him to rethink his agnosticism and accept there really was life after death and that for all his 70 years of doubt and disbelief his future had been and still was preordained. That for all his vaunted achievements, they counted for nothing with the guardians of Heaven and Hell. That to them he was an applicant lacking outstanding or redeeming features and as such was assessed a spiritual reject fit only to be consigned to limbo.

But most depressing of all was the realisation that if neither St. Peter nor the devil were convinced of his spiritual worthiness, then viewed objectively the sum total of his life was of no more significance than any run-of-the-mill human being. That for all his striving as Whitehall mandarin, borough councillor, law-abiding citizen, faithful husband, dutiful parent and member of the Queen of England's British Empire, he, Oliver Wilbur Trotter, was truly as the demon had accurately dubbed him – a mugwostic, a Mister Nobody!

CHE SARÀ, SARÀ

If ever there was a reason for me not to travel to Bangkok, or anywhere else for that matter, then Friday the 13th of January 2000 was that day. I'd overslept heavily, leaving me no time to follow my usual routine of driving to Heathrow and parking in a long-stay garage until my return from a business trip to the Far East. Instead I had to hire a minicab to take me from my home in Watford to the airport. Then the driver had a shunt on the M25 and police had to sort out the resulting traffic jam. To compound the nerve-racking experience, I arrived at the international terminal only to discover my passport and tickets were still in my briefcase on the back seat of the cab. There was a further nail-biting delay till the driver was located and redirected, by which time all other passengers on the scheduled flight had already checked in and were aboard the plane.

As I hurried after them I had an overwhelming premonition that these incidents presaged something untoward was likely to happen en route. During my career as an overseas sales director I'd experienced various crises on my travels. They ranged from planes dropping like stones in air pockets to lightning forking through fuselages on its way to Earth, and once over Tokyo Bay with a stuck undercarriage, when the pilot considered ditching in the sea rather than belly-flopping on land and bursting into flames. Fortunately, these dramas were avoided when at the last moment the plane's wheels lowered in time for touchdown. There were also two separate occasions when a passenger died in his seat, but I didn't consider either fatality counted as a crisis in the true sense of the word.

But this was the first occasion I had a feeling something

more significant was destined to happen and I thought of other calamities that could befall the flight and bring it to a grisly, untimely end. The plane's engines cutting out simultaneously leaving the aircraft to plummet into the ocean or territory we happened to be flying over at the time. The captain and co-pilot rendered unconscious with a deadly virus and no one aboard with flying experience to take over in the cockpit and the plane running out of fuel and crashing to Earth. Perhaps a terrorist displaying himself strapped with hand grenades and threatening to blow us all to kingdom come unless the pilot flew to Peru instead of the Yemen, or Russian MiG fighters appearing out of the blue and shooting us down for violating their military airspace. Then there were unpredictable natural disasters, such as a volcanic eruption sending impenetrable cloud thousands of feet into the sky, causing the plane's navigator to lose all sense of direction and finally crashing into a mountain. Or the plane disintegrating through metal fatigue and hurling everyone into the stratosphere before spiralling to Earth seconds later. There were also unexplained calamities when aircraft and passengers just vanished into thin air with the causes of their disappearance remaining mysteries to create the legend of the Bermuda Triangle. The list of disasters that could happen to flight Tango Zero Two with hundreds of passengers aboard was endless and all unbearably horrific.

In former discussions with friends and colleagues on the dangers of flying 33,000ft above the ground as compared to other forms of terrestrial transport, I consistently referred to myself as a confirmed fatalist. 'Che sarà, sarà' was my particular mantra on the subject of personal mortality. Dante Alighieri said 'What will be, will be' almost 700 years before they put his words to music. Now I wondered if perhaps I was being flippant holding this philosophy, that this morning was an example of what a person with common sense may have taken as significant omens and which I in my simple faith was failing to recognise. It was just possible that the failed telephone alarm call, the chaos on the Orbital Motorway and the mislaid briefcase were clear messages telling me not to catch flight Tango Zero Two to Bangkok.

As a result, I stood at the departure gates torn with indecision whether to go through them to the aircraft or return to the comfort and security of my suburban home. If I decided not to take the flight there was the question of delaying or cancelling prearranged schedules. There was also the embarrassment of explaining to boardroom colleagues precisely why I decided not to proceed. It couldn't be a fear of flying. 'Che sarà, sarà' I had claimed consistently. To admit otherwise was to destroy my fatalistic image forever. The only option left was to lie and say I'd been stricken with a viral infection of the debilitating type which afflicted the pilots in my fictional doom-laden scenario. It would be an excuse beyond challenge. Furthermore, if I telephoned 24 hours later to say the symptoms had moderated sufficiently for me to return to Heathrow and catch the next scheduled flight to Thailand it would indicate a devotion and duty to company matters way above that of fellow co- directors. Never in the history of commercial practice would abject fear have been put to such good use.

It was while considering these critical alternatives that a wildly unpredictable event took place to resolve my dilemma. I hadn't seen Louise Raynor since we parted five years before. There had been many occasions since then when I rued my unilateral decision to end our long passionate affair to seek and marry a more socially appropriate partner. Unfortunately for my choice of middle-class spouse, lovemaking was more a sense of dutiful coupling than physical enjoyment, and sexual intercourse with her never compared to that of my former lover who possessed a devotion to the joys of the flesh that defied description. There were countless times in the intervening years when I wondered if that fire still burned within Louise or whether she too had married and had her flames doused by domestic routine or even motherhood. Now as she hurried towards me at the departure gates looking the absolute picture of desirable femininity, there seemed no doubt in my mind as to the answer to that vital question. When she caught sight of me standing there she flung her arms around my neck in a spontaneously uninhibited and passionate embrace that sent my pulse racing and heart pounding. My joy was unalloyed. As the venue for a reunion of former lovers, Heathrow's international departure lounge was a perfect setting.

As we hurried to the aircraft arm in arm we discussed the incredible odds of our meeting and catching a plane bound for the same destination. All thoughts of doom and gloom completely vanished from my mind. Instead they were racing ahead to the possibility of rekindling our past torrid affair in one of Bangkok's luxury hotels. It was from that moment of anticipation that it occurred to me that far from the earlier obstacles put in the way of my reaching Heathrow on time being omens warning me against catching flight Tango Zero Two to Thailand, they were incentives urging me on to overcome them. From the very moment of our meeting at the gates to the aircraft it seemed crystal clear to me that Louise Raynor and I were destined to renew our passionate affair and if ever there was evidence to support my theory of life being preordained, today's events were proof positive of that philosophy.

On boarding the wide-bodied jumbo jet, it took a stewardess several tactful appeals to passengers to reorganise their seating arrangements so that Louise and I were placed side by side. As we strapped ourselves into our reclining seats I knew that before giving her any indication of my fervent hope of renewing our love affair there were niceties of social behaviour to be observed. We had to compare details of the way our lives had progressed since we parted five years ago. I was more than willing to admit that leaving her to marry my chairman's daughter as a calculated career advancement had been a major error of judgement. That within months of settling into a staid conventional union I realised it would have been better if I'd ignored the differences in our backgrounds which threatened to alienate me from family and friends and settled for those physical compatibilities that guaranteed an emotional and sexually fulfilling life together. The confession was good for us both. She held and pressed my hand all the time I spoke. I had then to discover what the intervening years had meant for her. Surreptitiously I looked to see if she wore a wedding ring but each finger was adorned with jewellery and I decided to wait to hear from her whether she was married or not. Simply judging by appearances it looked as if the passing years had been very kind indeed to my former lover.

Before Louise could tell me anything about herself there were the usual flight formalities that took priority over any intimate confidences. A chic and cheerful young stewardess demonstrated what life-saving equipment was available in the event the plane should come down in the ocean or how to put on a mask if the compartment we were sitting in ran short of oxygen. Then, when that duty was over, she hurried tail-wards only to reappear moments later pushing a drink trolley, and with that service completed, followed by dispensing breakfast trays and pouring tea and coffee. The whole routine was designed to take passengers' minds off the improbability of tons of metal plus hundreds of human beings defying gravity and being whisked into the stratosphere. As far as I was concerned, coping with a tray of pre-packed food and cup brimming with hot liquid was not the time to reminiscence with Louise Raynor about past pleasures, nor express hopes for a reconciliation and revival of them. For almost an hour into the journey there was no opportunity of expressing anything of a remotely romantic nature.

It was only when the food trays had been collected and we relaxed for the long journey ahead that she mentioned the reason she was travelling to Thailand. She held out both hands to display her collection of rings, then pointed to the trinkets dangling from her ears and finally to the chain pendant round her neck. With each movement she made I was aware of the ivory whiteness of her scented skin and pert attractive set to her fine features. The closeness of her had my senses aflame. She said because of the breakdown she suffered after my leaving her she was advised to find an occupation to take her mind off her unhappiness. As a result, she had found an outlet for her talents. It was designing decorative jewellery, having it made in Bangkok then selling it cheaply to friends who in turn sold it to their friends – in effect a commercial round robin. Operating with minimum overheads she was financially successful but added sadly that the material benefits were no compensation for the absence of any fulfilment in her private life. Hearing this I clasped her hand in a gesture of sympathy and from the warm response that flowed between us I knew for certain that when we reached Thailand and checked into our hotels we would soon after resume our intimate relationship.

For the remaining hours of the long flight there wasn't a moment when I gave thought to any of the dangers of travelling 33,000ft above the Earth's surface. I didn't worry if all the plane's engines faltered simultaneously or how long it would take to spin to the ground. I didn't study the appearance of every passenger in sight to see if he or she was prepared to blow everyone to kingdom come if the pilot didn't alter course and fly to where they wanted to go. Even the nightmarish possibility of the plane coming apart at the seams and after being decompressed into the atmosphere fluttering like a leaf to the ground remained far at the back of my mind. The anticipation of checking into a luxury hotel in the Thai capital and indulging in passionate sex with my former lover overrode all these latent fears.

And so at the end of the journey the longed-for wish came true. We checked into the same hotel and our lovemaking there proved even more passionate than when we last lived together. For the following days the only occasions spent apart were to keep our prearranged business appointments, neither of us wishing to be separated longer than was necessary. For my part, life in the exotic atmosphere of the Thai capital was indeed a many splendoured thing and the desire to remain in this euphoric state so intense I seriously considered staying on to lead a hedonistic existence far removed from family and friends. Five years before, I'd yielded to family entreaties not to abandon my social milieu nor thwart my career on account of Louise Raynor. That it was a serious error of judgement on my part to disregard the fact that she was an amoral female from a low and dubious background and the chasm between us such that the affair was doomed to fail. Their persistent arguments finally convinced me and I ended the relationship, only to discover that marrying within my milieu to a woman of impeccable morality was no guarantee of happiness or fulfilment. I soon yearned for the pleasures of my former lover and despaired of ever recapturing the physical delights of our life together. Now, by the merest of coincidences, the pipe dream had come true. It only needed my paramour's approval for us to abandon England and spend the rest of our lives in the joy of each other's company.

As I fervently wished, Louise Raynor was ecstatic in opting for a lotus-like existence far from my disapproving family and cynical contemporaries. Being exiles among the gentle Thais with no awareness of English class distinctions was an assurance for our happiness together. All that was required to achieve this state of nirvana was to return to London and with the greatest secrecy attend to essential financial details before making our final exit.

When we checked in at Bangkok airport to catch the scheduled flight to Heathrow, the London-bound plane was Tango Zero Two, with the same flight crew, which to me was further evidence of life's predestination and that everything augured well for the future. Whether over land or water, nothing would happen to the plane or its passengers. No one would be jettisoned into the air as the plane blew apart, no terrorists would divert it from its course to London. And without doubt there would be no approach for a volunteer to fly the plane because both pilots were in a coma from some deadly virus and the aircraft had to land before it ran out of fuel.

There was a repeat performance by the pretty stewardess rearranging passenger seating so that Louise and I were together and the routine duties that followed were as predictable and comforting as the quiet hum of the plane's engines as it cruised six miles up in the air. As I settled down for the long journey I mused on the circumstances of the past week. Whereas at the start of the journey to Bangkok I'd been fraught with anxiety as to Louise's reactions, on the return to London I was relaxed and contented. No one, certainly not myself, could have predicted the dramatic changes to my life as the result of a chance meeting with Louise Raynor at Heathrow's departure lounge. I thought of the reactions of my wife, family, friends and business colleagues as they read my farewell letters coordinated so that each were notified at the same time of my escape to happiness and delivered far too late for them to do anything about it. My future with Louise was the stuff of romantic fiction, of life imitating art. We were natural soulmates, our compatibilities transcended class or education. Social conventions or refined behaviour were of no account, only our physical and temperamental togetherness. Of equal importance, our combined capital, discreetly transferred from England and later astutely invested, guaranteed a blissful carefree existence together.

The landing at Heathrow was smooth and as we filed past the staff and disembarked they smiled and thanked each passenger in turn for travelling with the airline. I said I hoped to see them again on my next flight to the Far East as flight Tango Zero Two and its efficient crew were a credit to their employers. As we made our way along the walkway to passport control I automatically headed for customs' green channel. On my overseas visits I always travelled light and never brought back any item of value. For her part, Louise said she would go through the normal channel, as she was importing jewellery which was taxable, and leave its duty value to the assessment of customs officers. I was impressed and admired her for being a demonstrably honest citizen. She handed me her personal shoulder bag to make it easier for her to carry her case of samples and promised to reclaim it when we met up again in the passenger concourse.

I had no misgivings when I saw the two customs officers standing at the exit to the green channel. Nor when they requested I accompany them to their private office. It was, they said respectfully, merely a random check. True, the unguarded channel was for travellers with nothing to declare, but it was open to abuse from certain types of unscrupulous dishonest people. In turn I was tolerant and good-humoured. I said I appreciated they had their duty to perform and offered my briefcase for their inspection, but to my surprise they ignored it and asked if they might look into my shoulder bag instead. I thought it a very odd question and remarked it wasn't mine but belonged to my travelling companion who at this very moment was passing through their goods to declare channel and that I was simply carrying the holdall to lighten her load until we met up again in the concourse. Strangely, neither seemed interested in my explanation. Instead they were preoccupied rummaging through the contents of the bag, having tipped them onto their desk. I felt it was in order to protest at what seemed an invasion of private property. After all, I said, the bag only contained the usual paraphernalia of a young woman concerned with her appearance. For a second time they ignored me. Then one of the officers took a knife and slit the stitches at the side seam of the bag. I was angered at the wilful damage and said so, but without replying he thrust his hand in the opening and one by one pulled out polythene sachets packed with white powder until there was a pile of them heaped on the desk. I looked at the customs officers in silent amazement and they in turn back at me. It was only then that the horror of the situation dawned on me, although there was nothing threatening in either of their attitudes. They seemed to accept I was telling the truth and that the sachets of white powder which quite obviously contained illegal drugs had nothing whatsoever to do with me; that I'd never done anything illicit in my entire life to bring me into conflict with the law. They were still silent as my mind raced for an explanation that would convince them and free me from the nightmare situation. I said the most obvious thing that came to mind – an explanation only a completely innocent man could offer under such dire circumstances – that the bag must have been deliberately planted. That it might well have happened on the crowded aircraft and if they contacted my travelling companion waiting for me in the concourse and brought her to the office she'd confirm the bag wasn't hers at all. Within seconds the mystery of smuggling illegal drugs into the country would be cleared up to their complete satisfaction.

It was only when, instead of complying with my request to seek out Louise and clear up the situation, one of the officers asked if she was a long-standing friend or just a casual acquaintance that I realised the situation was becoming more complicated. I had no wish or intention of admitting I'd been her lover years before and recently revived the affair in Bangkok. Instead I claimed it was the chance seating next to her on the plane for the flight to London that accounted for the liaison and that the intimacy might not continue once we parted and went our separate ways from the airport. My version of events appeared to satisfy them. While one officer gathered Louise's personal items and packets of drugs and put them in a polythene bag, the other asked in the politest way if I minded accompanying them to confirm my version of events.

There was no suggestion of intimidation or officiousness by either customs officer. One even insisted on carrying my briefcase, which served as an overnight bag and weighed but a few pounds. To my surprise we didn't make for the concourse to reunite with Louise Raynor and clear up the matter of the holdall to their satisfaction, but to another section of the airport and eventually into an en suite bedroom and it was there that they left me. It was when a third customs official arrived and asked me to strip and took each item of clothing down to and including my underwear so that I stood naked before him, that with parched mouth and trembling body I asked what on earth was happening! I tried to sound outraged that such an indignity should be perpetrated on a UK citizen of impeccable character and in London's Heathrow Airport of all places, but instead of commenting he handed me a coarse cotton dressing gown and disappeared from the room. His emotionless response struck more blood-freezing fear in me than had he ranted at my criminal cupidity.

Left alone and isolated in the barely furnished room, I recalled a Kafka novel where an innocent man was persecuted and terrorised and never a reason given nor a purpose to the official tyranny explained or excused. I was in the depths of despair when one of the original customs officers came back into the room. He was as courteous and pleasant as before and seemed genuinely sympathetic to my harrowing circumstances. When I protested at the unwarranted indignity I'd been subjected to and questioned why I was being held in such offensively humiliating conditions, he explained that customs officers had a dilemma when discovering a passenger returning from abroad with a large quantity of heroin in his or her luggage and claiming to be unaware of the fact. They needed to be convinced they weren't smuggling illegal drugs into the country for criminal profit. I reminded him that I'd already given him and his colleague an assurance that the heroin or cocaine wasn't hidden in my personal luggage. That the bag I was carrying had to be the property of some unknown passenger who'd contrived to switch it with that of my travelling companion who in turn could not possibly have known of its illegal contents. My explanation had only to be verified by contacting the young woman with whom I'd spent a pleasant few hours on the flight from Bangkok and who in all probability was still waiting for me in the concourse, anxious to reclaim her personal belongings.

My further appeal for him to contact Louise Raynor had no more effect than when I first protested my innocence. It was at this point in the impasse that the taciturn official returned and still without a word of explanation held out a capsule. I looked in astonishment from his outstretched palm to the original customs officer who explained that drug couriers used many methods to hide their contraband. To be absolutely certain I wasn't carrying any more illegal powders on or in my person, it was a matter of routine to examine the body's cavities and internals. That was why it was necessary for me to accept customs hospitality for a free overnight stay at Heathrow Airport and submit to a body examination. He added that if a search of my anus or the contents of my bowels proved negative it would go some way to support my version of events and even count in my favour at a future criminal prosecution. It was quite obvious from the tone of his voice that he was sympathetic to my being subjected to this ignominious procedure and he waited while I swallowed the pill and until the other man left the room before continuing.

He said, going back to my story earlier on, that he and his colleague knew without bothering to look that Louise Raynor wasn't waiting for me in the concourse. She never was when any of her couriers were caught smuggling, pleading with customs officers to go find her and clear them of complicity. She was a regular drug importer and the designer jewellery operation was only a front to her real operation. It was a technique adapted to suit different circumstances, with Bangkok being only one source of supply. On this particular occasion they were more alert than usual because it was the first time she'd ever travelled with one of her couriers. Her last-minute meeting with me on the outward flight to Thailand and our stay together in a Bangkok hotel had never happened before. The stewardess of flight Tango Zero Two confirmed that Louise and I were known to one another and asked to be seated together so there was no question of our relationship being a casual one as I claimed. That as a result of this information in the few days available between our journeys, customs had time to make enquiries and confirm she and I had been lovers years before and only just resumed the relationship. To them it seemed obvious we'd decided to combine forces and under cover of our respective bona fide occupations expand our smuggling activities into an even greater illegal enterprise. It was only when she followed her customary practice of diverting attention and making good her escape that customs realised they'd been foiled yet again by her ingenuity; that I'd been used in the same way as her other decoys and contrived yet again to smuggle a quantity of drugs without being caught. The situation therefore was that while my body search was in progress, laboratory tests would be carried out on the confiscated sachets to confirm whether they contained heroin, cocaine or face powder. If they were Class A drugs then I would be in custody for a long time to come. Even if the contents were harmless, there could still be sufficient circumstantial evidence to bring charges of conspiracy to import forbidden substances against me. Either way, my situation was bleak and the future uncertain.

I listened, dumbstruck and incredulous, to the monstrous deceit Louise Raynor had played on me. Her carefully timed appearance at the departure gates and the passionate interlude that followed had all been meticulously prearranged. There was no lovers' agreement to abandon my wife, family and friends and spend the rest of our expatriate lives together – only a burning hatred and desire for revenge for my abandonment of her five years before.

The customs officer watched as I swallowed the pill and then lay back on the bed. I must have presented a picture of total despair as I stared up at the ceiling and reflected aloud on the bizarre sequence of events these past few dramatic days. I don't know what prompted me to take the customs officer into my confidence and expound my philosophy of life. Perhaps it was because all along he'd seemed sympathetic for the trap I'd fallen into and the personal ruination facing me. I mentioned the pre-flight obstacles that had almost stopped me catching Tango Zero Two and wondered if they'd been omens warning me against taking the plane or if, after all was said and done, my life was preordained and what happened was destined to happen. It's like the song, I said to him with a wan smile – 'Que Sera, Sera'. I took it for granted that he understood I was claiming our futures were written in the stars and there was nothing one could do about it. When I fell silent he looked at me with a slightly apologetic expression. He said he knew what

I meant about life being mapped out for us and it was all very well believing in Kismet, but wasn't it naive of me to believe in star-crossed lovers meeting by chance at a London airport and planning to start their passionate affair all over again? Shouldn't I have realised the women bore grudges for being rejected and discarded for someone else? He walked to the door and paused. I don't know about the song, he said, you'd have done better to remember the saying, 'Hell has no fury like a woman scorned'!

As he shut the door behind him I closed my eyes, and in the isolation of the customs hospitality room, for the first time since a child, shed tears and prayed for help. With a long, uncertain night ahead of me, I had time to relive the events of the past few days. While I knew for certain the purgative would prove negative, I was left agonising over whether Louise Raynor's holdall contained face powder or banned drugs; whether she'd planned to be content with my arrest and public humiliation or with venomous malice guaranteed my imprisonment for years to come. But that one way or another I'd spend my future either as a social pariah shunned by family and friends or incarcerated for years in one of Her Majesty's prisons. There was to be no sexual Utopia for me but an indefinitely enforced celibacy.

Flight Tango Zero Two had taken me to the heights and back again to the depths, but perhaps there had been another pilot who all along had been in charge of events. Maybe, just maybe, my future was written in the stars. Che sarà, sarà!

ACKNOWLEDGEMENTS

With thanks to Adam Stafford who loved Tony and the time they spent together reminiscing over past events. When the stories were discovered Adam read them all and helped to curate those we have published.

Thanks to Olivia Gallogy Clements who also read the stories and endorsed our selection. Thanks also to Eleanor Smith who has been a meticulous proof-reader and historical researcher.

Grateful thanks to Mark James for designing the cover that captures the essence of the first story.

A huge thanks to Jo James who as usual came up with just the right description for this eclectic mix of tales.

And finally, heartfelt thanks to my husband Barry, who edited some of the stories.

All of us have enjoyed Tony's insightful writing and the tales he has told. We hope new readers will be equally impressed.

Lightning Source UK Ltd.
Milton Keynes UK
UKHW020657080221
378420UK00013B/1093